In the summer of 17__, ____ ____ ____ ____ ____ ____ burly fisherman Robin Shipp live ____ ____ ____ ____ in a b____ ____ our town where most of the residents dislike him due to the ____ ____ f his father. With a hurricane approaching, he nonetheless convinces the villagers to take shelter in the one place big enough to hold them all—the ancient, labyrinthine tavern named the Moth & Moon.

While trapped with his neighbours during the raging storm, Robin inadvertently confronts more than the weather, and the results could change everything.

A NineStar Press Publication

Published by NineStar Press
P.O. Box 91792,
Albuquerque, New Mexico, 87199 USA.
www.ninestarpress.com

The Moth and Moon

Printed in the USA
First Edition
March, 2018

Print ISBN: 978-1-948608-14-5

Also available in eBook, ISBN: 978-1-948608-06-0

THE MOTH AND MOON

Glenn Quigley

To Ma. I told you I'd get round to it.

Acknowledgements

I'd like to thank Mark Wilson for his boundless love and support, Tony Teehan for his invaluable help and advice on the early drafts, and my mother, May, who has been patiently waiting for this for a very long time.

I'd also like to thank the people who made this book possible—my publisher Raeyvn McCann, who took a chance on me, my editor Jason Bradley, for his patience and encouragement, Natasha Snow, who designed a wonderfully striking cover, and all the team at NineStar Press.

Chapter One

MR. ROBIN SHIPP pulled his cap lower as he took a deep breath of salty morning air and watched the sun emerge from behind the headland. Stepping from the pier into his little boat, he ran his heavy hand across the prow, catching his coarse fingers on the loose, chipped paintwork. He picked a jagged flake off the wooden frame and held it up to the light, the vivid scarlet catching the pinks and oranges of daybreak. He let go and it drifted through the air, carried away on the gentle breeze, before settling on the soft, lapping tide. Most of the paintwork was in some state of distress. Deep cracks marbled the entire hull, belying the fisherman's profound affection for his vessel. *Bucca's Call* had seen better days.

"I'll paint you tomorrow, *Bucca*, I promise," he said.

He made this very same promise every morning, but every day, he found some reason to put it off. Before too long, he was humming to himself and hauling his well-worn oyster dredge over the stern of *Bucca's Call*.

"Beautiful!" he said as he emptied the net into a nearby tub. The shells clattered against one another as they fell. The boat bobbed about gently on the waves while gulls screeched and circled overhead. Her nameplate was missing a couple of letters and her white sails were truthfully more of a grimy beige these days, but she was as reliable as ever.

He was close to the shore and could see the whole bay—from the headland to the east, down to the harbour, past the pale blue-and-white-striped lighthouse that sat out at sea on its desolate little clump of rocks and scrub, and over to the beautiful sandy beach curving around and out of sight to the west.

The little fishing village of Blashy Cove sloped up the hills beyond the harbour, and with his gaze, he traced the low, stone walls lining each cobbled road. It was the only significant settlement on the tiny island of Merryapple, the southernmost point of a little cluster of islands nestled off the Cornish coast. The village had everything one would expect to find, except a place of worship. No lofty cathedral had ever been built there, no church of granite and glass, not even the smallest wooden chapel. When the empire of the Romans had fallen a thousand years earlier, its church had fallen alongside it. The invaders hadn't lingered long on the mainland, and had never set foot on these islands. Once they were gone, the people picked through the remains, seeing the value in certain aspects and thoroughly disregarding the rest, scouring the regime clean from the face the world and consigning it meekly to the tomes of scholars and students. In its absence, the old gods returned to their forests and deserts, their mountains and streams, their homes and hearths. Spirits of air and land and sea. Woden and Frig, The Wild Hunt and the Bucca, piskies and mermaids, the Green Man and the wights, all were changed, made kinder and gentler by their brief exile. On these islands, the old ways had been the only ways, but even these had mostly died out, sloping into traditions, superstitions, and habits. It was now August in the year 1780, and people believed in themselves.

At this time of morning, sunlight hit the brightly painted houses and sparkled on the gentle, rolling waves. The village's livelihood mainly revolved around the sea, but there was more to life than just luggers and lines and lobster pots. The Cove had long been a haven to those of a more creative bent. Painters and sculptors, engineers and inventors, they all found their home there. Some of them had come from the nearby Blackrabbit Island, which wasn't known for its love of the finer arts. This abundance of skill, and the nurturing of it, meant Blashy Cove had adopted some innovations not yet common in the rest of the world.

Robin had been out for some time by now and, as usual, had already eaten his packed lunch. Soon, his substantial belly rumbled and he decided it was time to head back to port. Packing away his nets, he heaved in his empty lobster pots, secured the tub filled with this morning's catch, and sailed the small craft homeward. As he did, he noticed a thin, grey line on the horizon.

"Looks like some bad weather on the way, *Bucca*," he muttered to the little boat.

The stern of the curious little craft sat low in the water, due equally to the weight of the morning's catch and the significant heft of Robin himself. While at first it appeared to be a traditional lugger, the kind of boat used by most fishermen in this part of the world, *Bucca's Call* was actually much smaller and faster, a one-of-a-kind built many years previously.

Huge ships from the mainland drifted past, their enormous sails billowing in the breeze. Merryapple was part of a small group of southerly islands, and the last sight of land some of the mighty vessels would see for weeks, or even months.

Merryapple Pier was the oldest one anybody knew of. The brainstorm of a local fisherman many years earlier and copied by many other villages since, it might well have been the first of its kind. This clever fisherman realised if there was a way for larger boats to offload their cargo directly, rather than having to put it onto smaller vessels to ferry back and forth between harbour and ship, it would increase the traffic through the little port. The pier stretched out past the shallower waters near the coastline. Little sailboats like Bucca's Call could dock right up close to the beach or even on the sand, if need be, while bigger fishing vessels could use the far end, in deeper waters. The pier was constructed from huge boulders hewn from the island's cliff face and supported by a framework of long wooden poles from the woodlands. In the evening, bigger boats from the village fleet usually dropped anchor in the bay, while smaller vessels stayed moored to the pier.

At the shore, some children were chasing each other around a pile of crab pots, hooting and hollering while May Bell finished her deliveries for the bakery. May was around the same age as the other children, but she was of a more industrious bent. She saw *Bucca's Call* approaching and ran to help Robin secure his mooring line as he lugged the tub of oysters onto the pier. When he clambered up the weathered stone steps, he steadied himself with a hand against the wall. The steps were wet and slippery, with dark green mould threatening to envelope his heavy boots should he linger too long.

"Morning, Mr. Shipp," the girl called as she finished tying the worn rope around an old, pitted stone bitt.

"Mornin', May! Thanks for your 'elp," he called back, waving to the girl as he lumbered past. Taller than any man on the island, he dwarfed the little girl, drowning her in his shadow.

"Time for food already?" she asked.

"Oh yes," replied Robin, "an' I know just the place to get some!"

His legs were stiff from sitting in the boat all morning. He knew he was supposed to get up and move around a bit every once in a while, but when he was out on the water, the chatter of the gulls, the lap of the waves, the smell of the sea air, it was all so relaxing he just didn't notice the time going by. Only his stomach growls marked the hours.

Mrs. Greenaway, wife of the village doctor and a friend of May's parents, happened to be passing by on her way home from the market. Seeing their exchange, she scrunched up her face, adjusted the bow on her bonnet, and seized the little girl by the arm, leading her away from the pier and avoiding Robin's disappointed gaze. He knew May from the bakery, as the master baker was one of his very few friends, but it wasn't uncommon for people to avoid him.

Robin heaved the awkward tub full of oysters up and marched towards the bustling market, which was a collection of simple wooden stalls selling everything from food to clothes to ornaments. He edged his way through the crowd, past various stallholders and shoppers as he struggled with the heavy container. Finally, he reached the largest stall, which sold all manner of fresh seafood, all caught in that very cove. Robin specialised in inshore fishing, whereas the other boats concentrated their efforts farther out to sea. He was one of only two oyster fishermen in the village. The other, Mr. Hirst, was ill and hadn't been out in his craft for almost two weeks. He was married, with a young family to feed, and the village had rallied around to help and make sure they didn't go hungry. The lack of competition, however, meant Robin was securing a bumper crop.

A tall, thin man in a white coat was scribbling notes onto a wad of yellow paper. In front of him lay a collection of various local fish, in everything from buckets to barrels to battered old copper pots.

"Got a nice batch for you this mornin', Mr. Blackwall." Robin beamed, holding up the tub so the fishmonger could get a good look.

"Yes, these will do fine, I suppose, Mr. Shipp. Put them down at the front." Mr. Blackwall was notorious for not getting too hands-on with the product or with much of anything, really. He kept his distance from the beach and fairly resented having to be even this close. Wet sand upset him greatly, as it had a tendency to cling to his shiny boots and sometimes it even marked his pristine coat. He didn't do any of the actual work with the fish, instead leaving it to his assistants. He'd often said he didn't see the point of having a stall at all when he had a perfectly good shop on Hill Road. But the market was a tradition in Blashy Cove, and so he had no choice but to participate or lose out. He jotted some numbers down on his paper and then chewed the end of his pencil as he tried to add them up. He always did this, and he never did it quickly. Robin stooped and laid the tub on the ground as instructed, grunting as he straightened.

"Joints sore again?" the fishmonger asked out of sheer politeness, not looking up from his calculations.

"No more'n usual," Robin replied, rubbing the small of his back and rotating his shoulder. Working the sea wasn't easy, and it had taken its toll over the years.

Ben Blackwall reached into his inside pocket and produced a fistful of polished coins, which he delivered into Robin's large, callused hands. Robin nodded appreciatively and stuffed them into the pockets of his calf-length, navy-coloured overcoat. Tipping his floppy, well-worn cap to his long-time buyer, he turned and headed away from the dock.

He passed by other villagers going about their morning routine and jumped out of the way of a horse and cart loaded with apples from the orchard over the hills as he headed straight for the immense building dead ahead. It was a massive, ungainly lump, set in the centre of a spacious courtyard, all crooked wooden beams and slanting lead-paned windows. Every now and then, a shabby bay window or wonky dormer jutted out at funny angles. It was hard to tell exactly how many floors it had. Five, at least, the topmost of which sat like a box that had been dropped from a great height onto the rest of the structure. Rumpled, uneven, and crooked, this odd addition had one large, circular window on each of its four walls.

On the ground outside, wooden tables and chairs were arranged, and heavy planters overflowed with hardy, perennial shrubbery. A couple of fat seagulls noisily argued over a few crumbs dropped near the windbreakers. This pair were here so often, they seemed to be part of the building itself. The locals named them Captain Tom and the Admiral. Captain Tom was the leader of a particularly noisy and troublesome band of gulls, and the Admiral was his main rival. They would often fight over even the tiniest scraps left on the ground, and both were marked with more than one battle scar.

As he pulled on the heavy oak door, the sign hanging overhead creaked and groaned in the wind. Painted on chestnut from the nearby wood, the bulk of the sign was older than the village itself, but it had been modified many times. Formed of several expertly carved layers, it now looked more like a child's pop-up book rather than the simple plank of wood it had once been. The overall effect was of peering through a forest, out over the cove at night.

The outermost tier resembled a ring of tree branches, gently moving up and down. Behind that layer were the turbulent waves, which clicked from side to side. Finally, there was the static crescent moon with a single cerulean moth flying slowly around, completing one revolution every hour. The whole sign ticked and whirred endlessly as its springs and cogs went about their work, and had to be wound up twice a day using a long, metal key kept tucked behind the tavern's main door. The name of the establishment was weaved around and through the artwork in gold.

This wasn't simply a place to drink or gather with friends; it was a place to conduct business, a place where people married, and a place where people mourned. It was a refuge from bad weather and jilted lovers. This was the heart and soul of the little village.

This was the Moth & Moon.

Chapter Two

ON HIS WAY to his favourite seat, Robin accidentally bumped into several different people, causing them to spill some of their drinks. This was typical of him. The slightest slip of his concentration and something was bound to hit the floor. He liked to chalk it up to him being far larger than the average Merryapple inhabitant, but everyone else knew it was just an innate clumsiness, which, after fifty years, he was clearly never going to grow out of. This tendency wasn't helped by the floor of the inn, as it undulated like the sea outside. One could hardly walk ten paces before being forced to climb or descend some little cluster of steps or other.

At this time of the afternoon, the perfume of the inn was a weak accord of tobacco and beer, swirled with the soot of candle smoke. It would intensify as the day wore on. When he reached a seat by the grand fireplace, he ordered a bowl of hearty crab stew and crusty, buttered bread rolls, which he devoured while listening to the gossip and chatter of the tavern folk. No one attempted to make conversation with him.

The tavern had been made from the wreckage of the first ship that ran aground on Merryapple. The bar itself was imposing and dark and sat on the ground floor of the inn. It was as if a separate entity had crawled into the middle of the Moth & Moon and now nested there, guarded by thick pillars at each of its corners and decorated haphazardly in lanterns hanging like offerings from grateful villagers to the sleeping beast.

A wide selection of glasses and tankards hung from the balcony overhead, and beyond the counter lay a series of walls and doors, some of which led to the kitchens deep in the bowels of the inn. The walls were decorated with display cases of various sizes and shapes housing the innkeeper's moth collection and shelves holding liquor of every kind. What hadn't been made locally or imported from Blackrabbit or the mainland, had been brought to the island by the many ships passing through. The selection on offer was unparalleled in this part of the world. Every type of whiskey, rum, gin, brandy, wine, and beer imaginable, plus a few other exotic drinks even Mr. Reed, the innkeeper, with his encyclopaedic knowledge of alcohol, would be hard-pressed to identify and reluctant to actually sell, for fear of unfortunate side-effects. The pride and joy of the drinks on offer was the locally made Merryapple Scrumpy, a very potent cider produced at the orchard over the hills.

Upon leaving the inn some time later, Robin walked past the heat and clamour of the forge and headed up the gently sloping cobbled street towards his home. Anchor Rise was a very steep, narrow road with houses on either side that ran up the slope of the headland then curved northwards and went back down again to join Hill Road. Robin's house was number five—a tall, thin building painted a dazzling white, like almost every other house in the village, but with a splendid sky-blue door. The house sat in the middle of a row of mostly similar-shaped houses, each one with a different colour front door. On one side of him lived Mr. and Mrs. Buddle, in the house with the red door. On the other side, with the orange door, lived Mrs. Caddy. The Ladies Wolfe-Chase lived in the mansion with the purple door at the top of the road. From the top floor of his home, on his bedroom balcony, he had a perfect view of the whole harbour, as the houses on the other side of the road were set lower than his. He could see clear across their rooftops to the harbour and bay beyond. Right now, though, all he wanted to do was soak in a hot bath.

He kicked off his heavy boots in the bright hallway and stood on the chilly little black-and-white diamond tiles in his thick socks. A toe poked through an extraneous opening, like a creature burrowing toward the light. Darning was another minor job he kept putting off. Sunlight poured through the multicoloured stained-glass porthole in his front door and showered the pale entrance in glorious hues of red, orange, and blue.

He hung up his overcoat on the wrought-iron coat hook affixed to the wall and stomped upstairs past a large oil painting of a stern-faced sailor with a short, wavy beard the colour of freshly cut straw. Dressed in a bulky coat, this seaman wore a flat-topped, navy-coloured peaked cap made from soft, braided cord, pulled low over his bushy blond eyebrows. Sewn to the cap by his father's own hand was a small anchor pendant with a curious quality—instead of being tied to a ring at the top, the rope emerged from a spindle in the crown. This was the very same cap Robin himself wore.

The round-faced subject stood proudly, with arms crossed, a brass spyglass clasped tight to his chest in one hand. In the pockets of this man's coat could be seen a journal and a compass. He was standing on the Merryapple headland, and behind him, heavy storm clouds were lavishly painted in thick, gloopy brushstrokes. In the distance, a mighty whaling vessel mastered the white-topped waves. The painting's ornate gold frame was wound in leaves and fish scales, and a small plaque at the bottom read "Captain Erasmus Shipp."

In his bathroom on the third floor, Robin turned on the brass taps and stoppered the plughole. The complex angular network of copper pipes snaking throughout his house, from the basement all the way to the top floor, rattled and gurgled and chugged as the piping-hot water came spilling out. This plumbing system was a bold experiment by some of the villagers many years ago and found extensively in Blashy Cove. Whenever he used it, he thought about how he used to have to bathe when he was a lad—in a battered old tin tub by the fireplace. He remembered how his father would carry the kettle from the stove and top up the bath with hot water, all the while humming some sea shanty or other. Sometimes, Robin caught himself singing those same tunes. He kept the old tub in the cupboard under the stairs, just in case these pipes ever stopped working.

The bathroom was white and panelled with long planks of wood. The great round frame housing the room's only window was painted in the same duck-egg blue he'd used elsewhere in his house. Like the rest of his home, the bathroom was in need of repair, especially around the curved feet of the bath where the regular overspill of water had worn away the paintwork.

He chuckled to himself as he plopped a little wooden toy boat into the water. It was a perfect replica of his own beloved *Bucca's Call*—complete with real canvas sails—made by someone very close to him and given to him as a present.

Well, they used to be close, at any rate.

He stripped off his clothes and dropped them into a wicker basket by the door of his bathroom. Now dressed in just his cap, he plodded into his bedroom and picked out an almost identical outfit—a heavy knitted woollen jumper, the same navy as his overcoat, a pair of long, cream-coloured linen trousers and a set of undergarments. Robin found little use for variation in his fashion, preferring instead to stick to what he knew worked for him. While he would occasionally replace an item of clothing if it became damaged or too worn to be of any use, it was usually with a near-identical piece. He would never dream of replacing his cap, however. He'd repaired it many times over the years, and it rarely left his head.

He carefully folded these clothes and neatly placed them onto a chair in his bathroom, beneath the round window with the same deliberate attention he gave even the smallest task. It was as though his every action, no matter how small, required the entirety of his concentration. When he was less than focused, things tended to drop. Or spill. Or break.

He oohed and aahed as he climbed into the steaming hot bath. It was a bit of a tight fit and some water tipped over the rolled edges and splashed onto the wooden floor. He was very tall, burly, and barrel-chested. "Stout" was the way Morwenna Whitewater always described him. She had practically raised him after his father was lost at sea. He had been ten years old then—almost a man, by his own reckoning—and defiantly claimed he didn't need any help, but every day, she would make her way down the hillside from her little cottage to make sure he was looking after himself. In later years, he had tried many times to convince her to take a room in his house. "You've looked after me long enough. Let me repay the kindness," he had said, but she was as independent as he was and preferred to remain in her cottage.

"Anyway," she had laughed, "I'd never manage all them stairs!"

Sometimes, it felt as if he was as wide as he was tall. He could just about lie down in the tub if he threw his broad, powerful legs over the end of it, which he did. His bulky arms and shoulders rested now on the edge of the bath. The model of *Bucca's Call* had quickly run aground on the fleshy island that was Robin's big, round, smooth belly. The water soothed his aching muscles, and as he breathed in the steam, he pulled his cap down over his eyes and lost himself in a daydream.

In the Moth & Moon, Mrs. Greenaway was talking to May Bell's mother and explained how she'd ushered the girl away from "that awful Mr. Shipp" earlier.

Mrs. Louisa Bell politely nodded along and made all the required frowns and clucks, but without any real conviction. Sensing she was being coddled, Mrs. Greenaway excused herself and ordered a cup of strong tea at the bar. She stood tutting to herself and shaking her head.

"You're too hard on that man, Mrs. Greenaway," said Mr. Reed as he handed over a small cup and saucer. Beside these, he placed a small ceramic teapot. Steam rose from its spout in gentle, silken eddies.

Mrs. Greenaway made a noise that sounded like *hrumph* and looked the little innkeeper in the eye. "He's a disgrace."

"He hasn't done anything," Mr. Reed replied calmly as he took the cloth from his shoulder and began drying some glasses.

"Not yet," said Mrs. Greenway, "but he already takes after his father in so many other ways; what's one more?"

She retired to a booth populated with other mothers, pushing her way onto a cramped bench.

"Remind me again—does your niece favour the cockerel or the hen?" inquired one of the women as politely as she could manage.

"She's not picky either way," replied Mrs. Greenaway, sipping on her tea.

"Well, that complicates things a little. Although the Undertons have a daughter who would be perfect for her."

"Oh no, she'd be far too old," said another. "What about the Trescothicks' son?"

Of all the tasks essential to village life that took place in the Moth & Moon, matchmaking was perhaps the most rewarding for women such as these. Unions with those from beyond the shores of Merryapple were begrudgingly accepted as a necessary evil at times, but on the whole, they preferred pairings were kept within their own community. For a brief time in the previous millennium, a peculiar restriction had been in place on the mainland insisting only couplings between men and women were to be allowed, and that anything else was immoral. Marriage was for the production of offspring, it was said. The people quickly rejected the notion, saying it reduced them to mere livestock. The decree had never taken root in Merryapple, nor on any of the other islands thereabouts, and it hadn't lasted long on the mainland either.

After his bath, Robin stood at the glass-panelled door to his bedroom balcony with a mug of hot tea in his hand and gazed out across the sea. His room was sparsely decorated with a dilapidated wardrobe that had seen better days, a chair sturdy enough to support his considerable bulk, a full-length framed mirror leaning against a wall, and a furry, white woollen rug. His hefty wooden bed had a little hook affixed to the side to hold his cap at night. The bed faced the balcony, allowing him to lie there and watch the sea, which he often did. A pile of books was stacked on the floor, each one with a tongue of paper sticking out near the beginning of the work, creating an angular totem pole of thirsty novels. A painting of a whaling ship at sea hung above his bed, the same ship as the one in the portrait of his father. The room was painted in his preferred scheme of simple white and blue, and it too needed some maintenance. The floorboards creaked and the paint had become distressed. Robin knew he needed to spend some time fixing it all up but kept putting it off.

Outside, the rolling grey clouds drew closer and closer. Setting the mug on a nearby shelf, he lifted a battered copper spyglass, opened the white door, and stepped out onto his little balcony. Through the tarnished and pitted glass, he spied the oncoming storm. Rain fell in hazy ribbons, and he thought he glimpsed the occasional flare of lightning. Muttering under his breath, he began closing all the storm shutters on his tall, thin house. A lifetime at sea had given him a keen understanding of the weather, and he felt in his bones this advancing tempest would be fierce. He grabbed his overcoat and cap and headed outside, and after quickly advising his neighbours to prepare for bad weather, he hurried along the cobbled road towards the inn.

He walked past the forge where the blacksmith's hammer clanged. Past the market filled with people haggling and gossiping. Past the little bay with boats rocking from side to side. Past the noisy gulls, still fighting over scraps. The wind was picking up now and the sky was growing darker. He hugged the huge lapels of his overcoat and drew it closer around himself. Inside the Moth & Moon, he spoke to the landlord and the customers.

"There's a storm comin', Mr. Reed. A bad one. Everyone should make preparations."

"You sure? Didn't look so bad earlier," George Reed replied, not even bothering to look up from the glass he was polishing.

"Well, go an' 'ave a look outside now," Robin said. "I think anyone who doesn't want to weather it at 'ome should come and gather 'ere."

"I don't think that'll be necessary..." Mr. Reed began.

He wrinkled his small, flat nose and rubbed his closely cropped beard. Everything about George Reed was short and compact. He had to have the floor behind the bar raised so he could comfortably work there. His hair was a mixed palate of colours, mostly shades of silver, blond and white, but tapering into a surprising near-black at the nape of his neck. His beard was silvery too, with a moustache the colour of the champagne he kept in stock but nobody ever ordered.

He mumbled something unpleasant about having his tavern filled with the whole village at once. Sometimes, the locals wondered why he'd ever agreed to run the Moth & Moon when he seemed to dislike being around people so much. He once told Robin how he didn't really have much of a choice, how his parents had run it since he was a boy, and his grandparents before them. After they passed away, he had taken over, though he could have sold it. Mr. Reed had mentioned he felt obliged to keep it in the family.

"Some of the older 'ouses might be damaged. And better safe than sorry," said Robin.

His accent had always been thicker than most, with a heavy emphasis on certain vowels. He put it down to the way his father spoke. Having been at sea most of his life and exposed to languages from all around the world, Captain Erasmus Shipp had fought hard not to lose his Blashy Cove timbre, and this had rubbed off on his son.

Mr. Reed sighed heavily. "I'll put the word round, Mr. Shipp, but I think you're worrying about nothing."

Robin walked outside, shaking his head. He stood facing the sea. The thin grey line had expanded into a churning, murky band on the horizon. He pulled his cap lower, as the wind blew harder.

"I'll get the rooms ready, just in case," Mr. Reed conceded.

Robin hadn't heard the short innkeeper approach, and started a little. They both returned indoors where Mr. Reed gave orders to his staff. Robin noticed Mr. Reed occasionally pausing midsentence and glancing sharply upward towards the darkest corners of the ceiling joists as if he'd spotted something untoward before carrying on with his instructions. These included asking the newest bar girl to tighten the laces of her generously filled blouse. The Moth & Moon had over two dozen rooms for rent, spread out across its many floors. The guests were usually sailors who revelled in the opportunity to spend a night away from the cramped confines of their ships. Robin spotted May Bell and asked her to go to Mrs. Whitewater's cottage and make sure it was closed up as much as it could be.

"Then bring 'er back 'ere. She'll argue and kick up a fuss, but don't you listen. Tell 'er I said I wanted 'er 'ere."

The girl turned to her mother, who thought for a moment, looking outside. Then she reluctantly nodded, and May went running at full pelt along the roadside. He dispatched another couple of lads to other elderly residents' homes with similar instructions and suggested to an attractive, well-dressed young man who had been leaning at the bar that he take his horse to the north of the island and warn the houses there. Archibald Kind was well known for his love of galloping around on his glorious steed, usually for the purpose of wooing some girl.

"Very well, Mr. Shipp," he said in his grandest tone of voice. "I shall convey word to those remote souls and return before the first drop of rain touches the cobbled stones of fair Blashy Cove."

He finished this response with a slight bow, a flick of his wrist and a flourish of his expensive-looking silk handkerchief, which he'd pulled unseen from his sleeve. Robin stared blankly at him for a moment, wondering who was supposed to benefit from this little performance. Then he noticed Mr. Kind hadn't really been addressing him at all, but rather the busty new bar girl who was standing behind him.

Robin set about helping the landlord close the inn's storm shutters. He grabbed one and heaved it shut, but true to form, he used entirely too much force and wrenched the heavy slated screen right off the wall. Mr. Reed stood and looked up at the fisherman with resigned disappointment in his eyes. Robin looked at the shutter, then at the hole left in the wooden window frame.

He smiled a big, doltish smile and said, "Sorry, Mr. Reed."

The innkeeper just sighed and walked off to find a hammer and some nails.

Once the shutter had been repaired, they and some other villagers present carefully removed the huge, ancient sign hanging above the main entrance and stored it in one of the rooms at the back of the inn. Extra blankets and bedding were tucked into corners for people to use on the benches and floors, in case the storm lasted a long while.

Robin then headed back outside to see what more he could do to help. He shifted plant pots and seating into the sheds at the rear of the inn, as well as anything else that might fly about in the winds and cause damage. When they were satisfied the Moth & Moon was ready, he set off to check *Bucca's Call* was safely moored and then went back towards his house, intending to make sure his neighbours were prepared. Word had spread, and he could see people hurrying about, locking horses up in stables and tying down carts. The market had been almost completely packed up already, and the stalls were being stored in a row of nearby sheds. The wind was really picking up now. Grey clouds were racing across the sea, bearing down like a giant wave threatening to swallow the village whole.

He didn't get very far before he saw a familiar face. A short, squat man with thick, wavy black hair and bushy sideburns. A pair of curious little, round, gold spectacles were perched on his snub nose. They had some extra, smaller lenses folded at the sides, each one connected to an individual arm and a series of miniscule joints. He was trudging along, hiding behind the collar of his sumptuous overcoat. Robin stopped in his tracks.

"Duncan. You've seen what's comin'," he said, nodding to the sea.

"I have," Duncan replied, keeping his eyes to the ground.

"Most of us are going to the Moth & Moon to wait it out. Do you...need any 'elp with your 'ouse? To get it ready?"

"No. It's fine. I'm on my way to close up the shop; then I'll head back home to get it sorted." He started walking again.

"Well, if you want to come to the inn, you—"

"I don't. I'm staying home."

"But—" Robin extended his hand.

"It'll be fine, Robin. I don't need... Just leave it," he called over his shoulder.

And with that Duncan Hunger trudged on towards the village's main street, leaving Robin to sigh and carry on back towards his own house.

Chapter Three

AFTER DUNCAN HAD walked away from Robin, he shook his head to clear it. Robin always seemed to bring out the worst in him. Duncan was quick to anger at the best of times, and conversations with that man, brief though they always were these days, had an edge to them that got Duncan's back up and made him defensive. He wished it weren't the case.

He scooted up towards his toyshop on Hill Road—the main thoroughfare of the village. Lined with timber-framed buildings, it was wide enough for a horse and cart, and not much else. Here and there, the upper storeys of some premises on both sides of the road jettied out at rude angles, almost touching at the bend where it turned into Ridge Street.

Every building on Hill Road was unique, but one stood out more than the rest. The Painted Mermaid Museum & Tea Room could be found on the corner and was a testament to the village's vision and commitment to art. The only gallery in the village, it was sea green in colour, drizzled—both inside and out—with fishing nets and seashells, and stuffed with paintings and sculptures and beadwork and crafts of all kinds. The windows were sculpted like portholes, and instead of curtains, long, twisted glass rods had been hung, each one a different thickness and different shape. These were slowly turned by the clockwork apparatus hidden in their pelmets, catching the daylight and reflecting it around the rooms, convincingly mimicking the patterns created by real waves and completing the illusion that one was in some fantastical museum at the bottom of the sea.

The owners were trying to cover the round windows of the gallery as Duncan opened the door to his own shop. It was filled with toys and games, all made by his own hand. Usually, the woodworking was done in the workshop at his home, and then he took the toys to the back room of his shop where he painted them. The toyshop was a panoply of colour.

A moving, swirling, undulating, bouncing, spinning cavalcade of animated toys. Suspended from the ceiling, a flock of geese flew round and round. On the floor, well-dressed monkeys banged their tin drums while pretty dolls waved from their cribs. Not every toy moved, however. A brightly coloured merry-go-round sat in the window, surrounded by boats of various sizes and shapes. Marionettes hung from the rafters by their controllers. Horse-drawn carriages rested on shelves, a row of ducks lined the massive cherrywood desk serving as his counter, and farmyard animals grazed on imaginary grass.

He hurriedly packed away any items that might be shaken loose and damaged in the storm and stopped all the wind-up toys. How quiet the shop became without the incessant ticking and clicking and clacking. He also took down the sign outside which read "D. Hunger Quality Toys & Games," and the wind chimes hanging from it. He shuttered the big, many-paned bay window at the front of the shop, and with one final check everything was in place, Duncan shut the door and dashed off towards his little blue house on the hill.

May Bell had raced out of the Moth & Moon and up the road towards a small row of cottages. She spent her whole life running from one part of Blashy Cove to the other. The wind was growing stronger, and leaves whipped past her. She reached the little iron gate of Mrs. Whitewater's tidy garden and undid the bolt. One neighbour was out in his own garden, gathering some tools and a basket that had been left lying. Another neighbour—a lightly built woman who seemed to be made entirely of tweed—finished beating a huge patterned rug with surprising force. She set the looped wicker carpet beater down, heaved the rug from the washing line on which it hung, and dragged it back indoors. May was put in mind of drawings she'd seen of a lion dragging away the carcass of a fresh kill.

On the wall beside the front door was mounted a small, circular stone carving of a man's face covered in leaves and framed by vines. The little girl knocked on the door, and Mrs. Whitewater called out to whoever was there to let themselves in. May politely entered the house.

"Little May Bell! This is a surprise. What brings you here?"

Mrs. Morwenna Whitewater was sitting by her stove, hands resting on her cane, as usual. She was a small woman in her late seventies with bright, vital eyes. Her short grey hair erupted from beneath her meagre bonnet and sat in loose, looping curls against her head. Quite round in shape, she usually wore a red shawl around her shoulders. The inside of her home would have been entirely unremarkable were it not for the abundance of paintings. Her late husband, Barnabas, had been a skilled artist, and every wall was covered in all manner of artworks, both framed and on bare canvas, some even painted on material like slate tiles or blocks of wood. From stirring lifelike portraits of local residents to still lifes to stunning landscapes and seascapes. Above the fireplace, in pride of place, was a modestly sized, framed painting of a young Morwenna and Barnabas Whitewater, made only a couple of months after their handfasting day.

May quickly explained how Mr. Shipp had sent her there to escort her back to the Moth & Moon for the duration of the storm.

"Oh, he did, did he?" Mrs. Whitewater sniffed. "Well, you can march right back there and tell him I'm staying where I am. I have plenty of food and wood for the fire. I'm not going anywhere."

May stood in the kitchen of the little cottage for a moment, uncertain of what to do. She could tell the old woman wasn't taking her seriously. Adults could get a certain look sometimes, one suggesting she was just a silly little girl and they knew what was best. She hated it, and she saw the look then as Mrs. Whitewater smugly neatened the folds in her own long, bluebell-coloured dress. May's hands clasped and relaxed a few times, and her mouth screwed up as she chewed the inside of her cheek. The grey clouds were moving ever closer. Finally, she took a deep breath, ran back outside, and slammed the storm shutters closed.

Mrs. Whitewater appeared at the front door, red-faced and flustered.

"Young lady, what exactly do you think you're—" she began but was interrupted by May walking right past her and back inside her house. There May picked up a straw basket and began filling it with items she thought might be needed. A bonnet, a tin of mints she saw on a table, and a small book.

"Excuse me, May Bell, but what. Are. You. Doing?" Mrs. Whitewater insisted.

May sighed and looked at the ceiling for a moment, composing herself.

"It's like this, ma'am," she said, tapping one foot impatiently. "Mr. Shipp gave me a job to do, and I'm not going to let him down. I know folks round here don't care for him, but he's always been very friendly to me and he seems like a nice man. He said you'd put up a fight, but I weren't to let you win. That you knew it was best if you come with me, and that he wanted you to come, and...well...let's go. Now. Please." She held the basket out.

Mrs. Whitewater looked at May. "Meagre of frame but ample of will, I see. Just like me at your age."

She took her coat from the back of the door and the basket from May and said, "Well, let's get going then. Musn't keep Mr. Shipp waiting!"

On Hill Street, the shopkeepers were finalising their storm measures. Mr. Buddle, the glazier, was securing his premises. Mr. Blackwall was back from the market and carefully stacking up his trays, making sure each pile was the same height and perfectly aligned. Mr. Bell was setting up a small ladder to remove his shop sign, while his wife, Louisa, fortified the windows.

Mr. Edwin Farriner was in his bakery, a few doors up. He'd been there since dawn, working nonstop, and had made almost all of his bread for the day. He was in the process of preparing for the following day when Mr. Blackwall had popped his head in the door and told him he was packing up for the bad weather and heading to the Moth & Moon. Edwin thanked the fishmonger and started packing up his flour and dough. He stopped the automated mixing apparatus—beautifully gilded clockwork machines for folding dough. He shook his head as he did so. He didn't know how long the storm would last, and he was unhappy at the thought of losing time when there was so much to be done already.

Upstairs in his living quarters, he made sure everything was locked down, then returned to the ground floor and quickly barricaded the windows. He packed a couple of trays with bread, buns, and cake and covered them with some cloth to protect them from the rain.

His bakery solidly secured, Edwin raced up Ridge Street and over the other side of the hill towards his parents' house, which was part of a row of houses beside the main road. Farther north, and slightly to the east, lay a large farm, founded shortly after the island was settled and still in the hands of the same family. Beyond that lay the north coast, where only a couple of houses stood. It was particularly exposed to the elements and home to only the hardiest of souls. He heard a galloping coming from behind him and instinctively jumped out of the way. Archibald Kind shot past on the back of Sweet Eclipse, his magnificent black horse. The ruffled collars of his extravagant shirt fluttered in the breeze, and his flowing hair trailed behind him like a silken tail. Headed north, Edwin assumed he was going to wait the storm out holed up in a barn, wrapped in the arms of a beautiful young woman. Or two.

Hurrying on to his parents' house, he found his mother and father already preparing for the coming storm. He set the trays of bread down on a table and hastily assisted his father in closing the shutters. His mother began fussing over him. She was a tough, wiry woman with wild red hair jumping off in assorted directions from her head.

"You're not stripped up for bad weather!" she cried.

Which was true; he wasn't prepared for rain at all. He was wearing his favourite cream linen shirt and sand-coloured breeches, with a tattered brown apron covering both. His only coat was lying in his living room in a state of disrepair. He'd caught it on a loose nail and ripped one of the arms quite badly.

"Come upstairs. I'm sure I have something old of your father's you can wear," his mother said.

"I told you we should have kept some of Ambrose's clothes, Sylvia," his father said from the doorway.

"No one asked you, Nathaniel," his mother said sharply. His father sheepishly ducked back outside again. Edwin was big and broad-shouldered with a strong chest and a stomach that was getting softer by the day. His father, though a little stooped and frail these days, had a similar physique in his day, and his mother said she was sure she had something from her husband's youth that would fit Edwin.

"Mum, there isn't time for..." Edwin started, but his mother held up a wrinkled palm and he fell silent. He knew better than to argue the point.

She riffled through some clothes in a wardrobe while Edwin shuffled around the dim, untidy room. She pulled out one jacket, a heavy woollen grey number with brass buttons and held it up to Edwin's chest. Finding it entirely too small, she returned it to the rack and kept looking. Edwin perused the clothes on offer and touched upon some emerald green item at the back of the wardrobe, with dented and tarnished buttons. His mother slapped his hand away.

"That's no use to you, unless you want to wear a ladies jacket to the Moth & Moon!"

"Well, you never wear it. Anyway, it might look quite fetching on me. Bring out the colour of my eyes," Edwin joked.

His mother rolled her own piercing green eyes and after some more searching found a mushroom-coloured frock coat decorated with gold filigree. It was old-fashioned and far more formal than was necessary. Edwin slipped the coat on and though it was quite snug, it would have to do.

Once downstairs, he lifted the trays of bread and tried to coerce his parents into joining him at the inn.

"No, we'll stay here and look after the house," his father said.

His mother crossed her arms and squinted.

"I suppose your 'friend' will be there," she said with obvious unguarded contempt.

Edwin sighed, feeling deflated. This again.

"Yes, Mum, Robin Shipp will be there. I hope that's not why you're both staying here?"

His father rolled his eyes and shrugged his shoulders as if to say it wasn't his choice.

"No, no, we just feel we're better off here," his mother said.

"Well, if you're sure."

Edwin leaned down to kiss his mother on the cheek. She smiled, but he knew it was put on for his benefit, to show him that she was fine. He wasn't convinced, but he knew better than to argue.

Dashing back towards the top of the hill, Edwin couldn't help but notice the aroma of the bread he carried as it mixed with the delicate scent of apple blossoms. Once he crested the hill, those sweet bouquets were replaced with the rather more lively smells of the harbour. Fish, salt, and straw. Every time he crested these hills, which circled Blashy

Cove and hid half of the village from the rest of the island, he was struck by how the rustling of the trees in the orchard and woods to the west was replaced by the crashing of the waves. As a boy he'd misspent many a summer's afternoon in those woods, playing in the old walnut treehouse overlooking the graveyard and raiding apples from the orchard. Nowadays he used that same orchard's fruit to bake pies and tarts for the village, using recipes handed down from his grandmother to his father to him.

At the top of the hill, he stopped for a moment and surveyed his surroundings. From there, he had an unobstructed view over the village right down to the harbour. He could see as far as the headland to the east and the fields to the west. And also the immense clouds bearing down on the village. They rolled and churned, flowed and swirled, a reflection of the angry waves below. They galloped toward the village with menacing purpose, expelling gallons of rainwater as they went. The sea was above them now, and it was coming to drown them all. Edwin had lingered too long and ran towards the Moth & Moon.

Robin had returned to the inn. Some of his neighbours had refused his offer of help and began preparing for the bad weather in their own way, but the tavern was filling up fast. Almost every little alcove and table had someone seated there. The oldest faces were painted with concern, the youngest with excitement. The children didn't really understand what was happening, of course. They just knew a gathering of this many people meant a chance for lots of fun and games. They ran around in boisterous packs, weaving in and out of groups of adults and the posts holding the ancient ceiling up. Eventually, attempts were made to confine them to the rooms towards the back of the inn. Some had brought games and dolls to play with, and more than one tea party was already in progress.

Perched by the fireplace, in shawl and bonnet, sat Mrs. Morwenna Whitewater.

She had taken the prime spot at a large table. With many of the other elderly women of the village gathered around her, she was very much the King Arthur of this particular round table. Some of her vassals included Mrs. Greenaway—the wife of the village doctor—Mrs. Buddle, and Mrs. Caddy—who lived on Anchor Rise and had come here straight after receiving his warning—and her own neighbour, the tweed-clad carpet beater. Her name was Mrs. Hanniti Kind and she knitted with a ferocity unmatched by mere mortals. The incessant clacking of her knitting pins was mercifully drowned out by the general din of the assembled crowd, but Morwenna often said her vigorous rubbing of the wooden needles might one day set off a spark and burn the Moth & Moon to the ground. As Robin approached, Mrs. Greenaway and Mrs. Kind tutted audibly, earning them a cautioning glare from Morwenna.

"Well, Robin," she called. "Here I am."

"Hullo, Morwenner," he said. His heavy accent meant he always ended her name with an *er,* which he knew annoyed her a bit, but try as he might he couldn't help it. "I 'ope you didn't give young May too much trouble." He laughed as he bent down to kiss Morwenna's cheek.

May, who had been ordered to stoke the fire into a further fury with a long twisted black poker, turned and gave him a knowing look.

"Of course not, I came along quietly. I know better than to argue," Morwenna said, sniffing defiantly and adjusting her cane.

Robin went to speak to some of the men at the bar. Among them were Mr. Ben Blackwall and the local butcher, who was a very rotund man named Mr. Hamilton Bounsell. They thanked Robin for his warning, the first to do so. As he chomped on the end of a clay pipe, the butcher told the gathering that everywhere in the village had been boarded up, and all of the shopfronts were secured. Most of the villagers had gathered in the Moth & Moon.

They began to talk of buildings that might not survive. Mrs. Whitewater's cottage was mentioned, as was the schoolhouse and a couple of homes near the seafront. Someone mentioned Duncan Hunger's house on the hill, but Robin told them he'd spoken to him. There was a leery silence at that, and just as Mr. Bounsell was about to break it, all colour quickly drained from the world. Living at the coast, the people of Blashy Cove were well used to bad weather. The village was nicknamed Rainy Day Bay, after all. They had even laughed and joked as they made preparations for the storm, but now the wind suddenly began to howl and thunder exploded in a deafening chorus of fearsome roars.

The storm had arrived.

Chapter Four

THE LANTERNS HANGING from the walls of the Moth & Moon flickered in the hush that followed. Everyone held their breaths as they listened to the tremendous crashing and banging outside. The masts of the luggers docked in the harbour rattled and clanged. It was very difficult to see outside as the clattering storm shutters covered every window, but it was just possible to see through some cracks and gaps. Every now and then, almighty snapping, rending, fracturing noises sounded as the roofs were torn off buildings. This storm was going to be worse than they feared.

Edwin Farriner had arrived a few minutes earlier, dripping wet but otherwise none the worse for wear. He handed the trays of bread over to Mr. Reed, explaining he'd brought them in case they were trapped in the inn for longer than expected. He knew the Moth & Moon often baked their own bread in the kitchens, but he thought every little bit would help. Edwin kept one loaf of his famous fruitcake aside and quietly gave it to Morwenna Whitewater's table of village elders. He winked as he placed the wrapped cake on their table, and many coos and oohs were heard in appreciation. Every one of the women was a regular customer of his, and he wanted to make sure they were comfortable and looked after. He spotted Robin and started off through the crowd to join him.

The Moth & Moon was the oldest building in the village. Cavernous, sprawling, and dark, it had been added to many times over the years, making it a labyrinth of rooms and corridors. Black wooden beams criss-crossed almost every surface. Lanterns hung low on the walls, casting a shallow light across the tavern. Various bric-a-brac, from irons to watering cans to flails and more than a few pieces of rusted fishing equipment, could be found on every shelf. The walls were either white, uneven, and limewashed, or dark panelled wood. Whatever their construction, they were punctured with niches of varying sizes filled with candles or books or tankards or far more colourful items. It was something of a ritual for sailors passing through to place a token in one of these hollows. Statuettes of outlandish, long-abandoned gods and demons were a popular choice, as were seashells from distant beaches. Necklaces, knives, and coins were dotted about like barely hidden treasure, each one a donation from a thankful visitor.

Some walls held framed paintings depicting various scenes of mighty warships blasting cannons or enormous whaling vessels crashing through vicious waves. One of the paintings, hanging in a dim alcove under one of the main staircases, showed four mighty ships engaged in combat in the waters of Blashy Cove. It was titled *The Battle in the Bay* and had been painted many years earlier by Mrs. Whitewater's late husband, Barnabas.

The ceiling over the bar and the main seating area was open to the second floor, and people gazed down from the railings every time the main door swung open. The giant ship's wheel serving as the inn's main candelabrum filled the air between the floors. It hung perfectly motionless, suspended from iron chains fixed to great beams in the ceiling and was caked in wax. Layers and layers of it. One could watch a fresh layer crawl over the old, a miniature tide slowly spreading to the edges of the wheel and dripping onto the floor below. Everyone knew where to steer clear of sitting or walking to avoid these molten dribbles. It was said that if someone were to excavate the wheel's strata, they'd discover tiers stretching back to the dawn of life of the island.

Occasionally the second floor inhabitants called and waved to the newcomers, and beckoned them to join them upstairs. There were candles lit on every table in the tavern, most in small brass holders or lanterns, but more than a few were set on a surface and held fast with their own wax, which flowed slowly over the edges in frozen falls.

As he went to join his friend, Edwin encountered a small group of people by the front door. A small, frail-looking woman was pacing up and down, clearly agitated. Some of the other villagers were trying to calm her down.

"But what about Jim and Allister? They've not come back yet. They took the boat out this morning and they've not come back yet!" She was becoming increasingly panicked, her voice rising, her eyes wide.

Edwin caught Robin's attention and beckoned him over. Mr. Bounsell was consoling the woman.

"Don't fret, Arabella," he said. "Jim's been sailing longer than any of us, I'm sure he's safe. He probably took to Rumbullion Bay, anchored down to wait out the storm. There are caves there, lots of shelter. Don't you fret now, go and have yourself some tea."

Two of the older woman's friends had joined the group, and one of them carefully placed an old, knitted blanket around her shoulders and led her back to the big table by the fire where many of the mature women of the village had gathered, lorded over by Morwenna Whitewater and her cane. A fresh pot of tea and a slice of fruitcake were waiting for her, and Arabella Stillpond looked calmed.

Mr. Blackwall gathered the men closer together. Robin stood behind them. Not excluded, as such, but far from welcomed.

"Do you really think that's what happened? You think old Jim went to the Bay?" asked Mr. Blackwall.

"He might've done. If he didn't make it back here, it's the most likely spot," Mr. Bounsell said.

Robin looked concerned and cleared his throat as if to speak.

"What do you think, Mr. Shipp?" Edwin asked, offering him a way in.

Robin leaned in to the circle a bit. "The trouble is those caves fill up fast. 'opefully, Jim and Allister retreated far enough into them before the water level rose. They won't 'ave stayed on the boat. Even anchored it would be a risky prospect in this weather. Soon as the storm passes we'll 'ave to send a party out there to check."

Robin's voice was naturally gruff in tone but friendly in manner and could be very comforting when he remembered to take the harsh edge off it.

"Assuming any of the boats survive..." Mr. Bounsell said.

There were a couple of rowboats in a shed by the water that should be unscathed. These were smaller even than *Bucca's Call*, but Mr. Bounsell's point was a good one. No matter how well prepared they were, weather this severe could easily damage the village's entire fleet.

Mr. Reed was walking around with a tray of tankards, still gazing upwards every now and then. Several times he almost tripped over some children, and once his own feet.

Edwin and Robin made their way upstairs to one of the spaces at the rear of the building. The staircases in the Moth & Moon were winding, twisting affairs and they often doubled back on themselves at sudden, awkward angles. They were peppered with landings, big and small, some of which could barely hold one person, while others held entire tables and chairs. Low-ceilinged and tucked out of sight, these little hidey-holes were the most favoured of patrons wishing a modicum of privacy. The staircases riddled the whole building, cropping up in the most unlikely places and never continuous, meaning a person who reached the end of one and wished to keep going was forced to hunt for the next one on whichever floor they found themselves. To make matters worse, there was always more than one staircase to choose from, making the Moth & Moon something of a vertical labyrinth. People who knew the place well would still find themselves having to stop and get their bearings every once in a while, so it's no surprise newcomers—guests who would stay for only a night or two—could often be found wandering the halls at night, having gotten completely and thoroughly lost on their way to or from their room. The alcohol probably didn't help.

Edwin and Robin wanted to see out to the village, and the four large, round windows on the top floor offered the best views. These had shutters on them, of course, but they were by far the most weathered and had the biggest gaps in them. Being that they were the highest points on the building, one facing in each of the cardinal points of the compass, they were the most infrequently repaired. The glass was ancient and thick, with big dollops where it seemed to be dripping slowly toward the ground, and set with lead framing. By the time they had manoeuvred their way through the esoteric layout, they were a little out of breath. They sat at the north-facing window and squinted, trying to get the best view, while Robin rubbed at his knees, as he so often did. Whenever Edwin asked him about it, Robin just said they were "actin' up a bit" and not to worry. The bench at least was cushioned, and the window sat out in a roomy, arched, wooden bay.

Edwin pointed up to the eaves where they could just about make out the plump feathery forms of Captain Tom and the Admiral sheltering on a beam jutting out, forming a little dry rest spot for the birds. In the cramped conditions, they occasionally pecked at each other. Edwin wondered if the same might happen with the villagers packed in the tavern. Tensions could run high in close quarters.

It was gloomy now, and the rain was the heaviest they'd ever seen, but it was just possible to make out some of the buildings in the village beyond.

"Robin, look," Edwin said. He pointed to Mrs. Whitewater's cottage. The roof was almost completely torn off.

Robin sighed heavily and shook his head. "'Ow many times 'ave I put off repairin' Morwenner's roof?" Edwin found the mispronounciation of her name delightful.

The schoolhouse was intact, so far, but some of the shutters hadn't been fixed securely and were clattering in the high winds. The glass in some of the windows was smashed. Slate tiles were flying past the windows, dozens of feet in the air.

"Well. I think it's clear now. This isn't just a storm. This is an 'urricane," Robin said with furrowed brow.

Chapter Five

FROM THE FRONT window of his little blue house on the hill, Duncan gazed down across the harbour as he lifted a fine china teacup to his lips. Rain ran in torrents down the glass. To his left, he could just about see the steep roads that formed the main part of the village, where every house and shop was locked down for the weather. Across the field and down the hillside was the schoolhouse, where earlier children had been excitedly running around in hats and scarves, delighted at their unexpected premature dismissal. At the old cottages on the far side of town, some older children had helped the elderly residents close up their homes, and guided them down to the Moth & Moon, where people were gathering to wait out the storm. The bad weather obscured that side of town from his vision now. Only vague, grey shapes were visible. Ghostly outlines in the distance.

The boats in the harbour tipped from side to side in the growing winds, and the waves splashed high against the lighthouse sitting on its tiny islet in the bay. He knew the keepers would be entirely isolated for the duration of the storm. The only way to access the islet was by sea, which would be impossible in the choppy waters of the storm. The keepers lived for months at a time at the lighthouse, but there was a difference between choosing not to leave a place and knowing you couldn't.

He considered taking up Robin's offer of sheltering in the Moth & Moon, but his house had stood for many years, long before Duncan had ever lived there, and this storm wouldn't get the best of it. It would be nice to have some company for the duration, though. Part of the reason he loved his home so much was its relative isolation, but having grown up on a farm, he was used to being surrounded by activity, and every now and then, he missed having some life around him. He finished his tea and went back to barricading all the windows at the rear of the house and in the small workshop.

The walls of Duncan's home were decorated in a rich forest-green wallpaper, swirled with ornate patterns of what appeared to be gold peacock feathers. His furniture was dark walnut wood, most of which he'd bought with the house. What he hadn't bought, he'd made himself. The trees north of the village were mostly walnut, cherry, and chestnut, so good quality wood was easily available. The previous occupant had died and left everything to his only family member—a distant cousin on Blackrabbit Island—who wanted to sell the house quickly and be done with it. A sideboard, writing desk, and cabinet sat in this room, and a giltwood mirror hung above the fireplace. On the mantelpiece sat a collection of small items he had carved. A bird, a cat, and a boat sat at one end, and a sleeping dog at the other. There was a thick-trunked four-poster bed and a spacious wardrobe in the bedroom. Everything had its place, carefully thought out and tested; everything had a purpose, either practical or emotional. Everything was just so.

Duncan had come to the village with a trunk full of clothes, a set of tools, and some money which he used to buy a house at the start of Anchor Rise. He began making toys and games from driftwood he'd collected on the beach and then selling them every morning at the market down by the harbour. He'd soon saved enough to buy permanent premises on Hill Road. Robin had been a great help and support through those early days. While this was a friendly village, he had come from Blackrabbit, and having someone vouch for him so early on, even someone with a reputation like Robin Shipp's, certainly helped Duncan gain a solid foothold.

Not long after he'd first opened his shop, he spotted a sublime coat at the market. A passing trader was setting up for the day, and there on his stall was a rich midnight-blue overcoat, inlaid with the finest gold thread, which swooped and swirled around the edges in mesmerising, intricate patterns. He'd fallen in love with it at first sight but, sadly, was unable to afford it. Some days later, he awoke to find it hanging on the coat hook in his hallway, with a note saying *Because you deserve it*. Well, what it actually said was *Becose you diserve it*. Robin hadn't spent much time learning to how to write as a child, preferring instead to be on the water as often as he could.

Robin explained how the coat would add to the atmosphere of Duncan's toyshop and his role as toymaker. A touch of showmanship and luxury. Duncan looked magical in it, and to the children of the village, he was something of a magician with his ability to create the most amazing toys from lumps of dead wood. Duncan revelled in this image, truth be told, and he still wore the overcoat, despite the memories it had come to embody. Also, unknown to everyone but himself, he kept Robin's note tucked at the bottom of the inside pocket.

After he and Robin had parted ways, Duncan sold his house with all its meagre furnishings and moved to the opposite side of the village, which was as far away from Robin as he could get while still being in Blashy Cove. It was a gesture he knew would hurt Robin deeply, though if Duncan had chosen the house on the hill specifically for that reason, he would never admit it.

Chapter Six

EVERY NOW AND then, a flash of lightning lit up the village. It afforded Robin and Edwin a momentary glimpse unencumbered by the rain and murkiness. The storm was already wreaking havoc, and it looked to Robin as though huge chunks had already been torn out of the Painted Mermaid. He wondered if the museum—home to island artefacts and artwork stretching back generations—would survive.

They sat facing each other now, each with a leg up on the bench and their backs resting against the sides of the arched window bay. Robin's eyes kept darting towards the little blue house on the hill, where he saw a faint light glowing behind the shutters.

"I'm sure he'll be fine, you know," said Edwin, following the direction of Robin's gaze to the house with the workshop at its side. "Though I do wish he'd come here with the rest of us."

Robin looked at Edwin for a moment. His instinct was to deny he was worried, but the two had been friends for some years now and Edwin knew him better than that. Robin sighed.

"So do I. If 'e doesn't come 'ere because of me, and anythin' 'appens to 'im..." He absent-mindedly rubbed one of the lobes of his little ears, as he always did when he was worried.

"You know what he's like—he wouldn't have come here anyway. Stubborn old goat." Edwin smiled over at the big fisherman next to him. His ever-present cap was pushed back, revealing his bare, wrinkled forehead and the single little tuft of white hair that had once been blonde. The look of worry on his face was unmistakable, however much he tried to hide it.

When they returned downstairs, they discovered many of the villagers who had sought to brave the storm in their homes had given up on that folly and journeyed to the Moth & Moon. It hadn't been easy going, and some had suffered injuries ranging from cuts and bruises, caused by fragments blown about in high winds, to broken limbs from falling walls, misjudged steps or—in one case—a frightened horse kicking wildly.

Edwin's parents were among the recent arrivals. They stood warming themselves by a small fire towards the rear of the tavern. Sylvia Farriner had refused to approach the main fireplace while Morwenna Whitewater held court by it, so she and her husband huddled around the little flames, trying to dry their soggy clothes.

Archibald Kind had returned with the residents of the north coast. Only three people lived in those remote homes—an elderly man named Oliver Cook, who had a long flowing white beard and lived alone, and a couple named Tobias and Rosanna Trim. They feared what would happen if they remained in their ancient houses, so they gladly took Mr. Kind's advice. They packed some sacks with provisions, barricaded their homes as best they could and returned to Blashy Cove with him. With their horses tied up in nearby stables, they settled in for the duration.

A panic was setting in amongst the crowd. May Bell was missing. Against her mother's wishes, she had sneaked off to encourage her stubborn uncle to come to the inn. She was successful in convincing him, but her uncle had just arrived at the Moth & Moon without her, and said May had left some time before him. May's younger brother suggested she might be sheltering in one of the old boats down by the beach as they often played there. Everyone knew which one he meant—the largest of the derelict rowboats sat on its side, half-buried in the sand. It leaned away from the sea so would offer some protection from the storm. That particular rowboat had been there before their grandparents were born, and a popular story claimed it was a lifeboat from the original ship that settled the island, though in truth, it came from much later.

The girl's parents were beside themselves with worry. Her father, Henry, had injured his ankle earlier in the day. While he was on a stepladder shutting up his shop, a gust of wind had knocked him over, and he landed awkwardly on it and had to be helped to the inn by some neighbours. He said he'd be able to go and search for his daughter just as soon as Dr. Greenaway arrived and fixed his ankle.

Robin wondered if perhaps the storm would pass quickly and there would be no need for anyone to search for her. Perhaps the rain would simply stop and May would emerge from her shelter, damp but in good spirits. Then he thought of Morwenna's roof, strewn halfway across the village. As the wind howled and rattled the old inn, he accepted there was no time to lose.

"We can't wait," he said at last.

He grabbed his heavy overcoat from the crowded hooks by the doors and a lantern from a table, pulled his cap down over his head, and made for the door. Sylvia Farriner slid her way through the crowd, presumably for a better view of what was happening. She drew the still-damp grey shawl around her delicate frame and made some attempt to smooth her untamed red hair into shape. Her husband obediently traipsed along behind her like a lapdog.

"I'll come with you!" Edwin shouted as he went to collect his coat.

"You will not!" his mother wailed, positioning herself between her son and the crowded coat hooks. "It's too dangerous out there; your father almost broke his neck on the way here."

"You stay 'ere and be ready to open this door," Robin replied. He thought this little discussion was wasting precious time, and he'd rather Edwin stayed out of harm's way.

"Let the lout go," said Sylvia Farriner, eyeing Robin contemptuously. "No sense two of you risking injury."

The door swung violently open and Robin disappeared into the rain. He made his way carefully in the direction of the beach, finding it hard to catch his breath. Several times he lost his footing and crashed to the slick cobblestones with a mighty thud. It was getting dark by then, and the debris flying through the air made things especially treacherous. Stopping to take shelter behind an old shed, he checked he was heading the right way. The shed shook and rattled and seemed set to fly apart at any moment. It was used by the Moth & Moon, and across the courtyard, toward the small pathway and the hill beyond, were a row of similar sheds used by the fishermen to store equipment and the market stalls. He hoped these would provide some shelter. When he finally reached them, after falling a few more times, he found that they did. The wind roared round them, stealing the breath from his lungs, but the structures offered some momentary protection from the airborne fragments scratching his face.

He was already drenched from the driving rain. It took him some time to reach the beach. While he knew this village like the back of his hand, it was extremely difficult to see where he was going in this weather, and the wind had carried him off his feet several more times. The glass panes of the little lantern had already cracked, and he kept it close to him to protect the flame. In the distance sat the hull of the rowboat. But only one. The others were gone, snatched away by the grasping tide. Lightning crackled overhead, and the thunder shook him to his bones. All he could taste was seawater as it blew across the beach and onto his gritted teeth. The waves were getting closer and closer to the hull of the boat. Soon, they'd engulf it completely, and the girl would either be smashed against the rowboat or pulled out to the sea. Robin waited for the waters to recede, then flung himself onto the beach. As he did, he hoped May really was under the boat, or he risked being trapped himself.

Wet sand clung to his boots and the bottom of his soaking-wet overcoat as he struggled towards it. Finally, he reached the rotting rowboat and threw himself behind it. He almost frightened the poor girl to death. The rain pounding on the hull of the rowboat was deafening, and water poured in where clumps of wood had rotted away. May had been crouched there, with her hands over her ears. She recognised him and hugged him immediately. He wanted to rest for a moment, but the lightning was becoming more frequent, and if anything, the rain was getting even heavier. The high winds and howling rain made it pointless to talk. He gestured to her that they had to leave, but she was frightened. He took his cap from off his head and plonked it on hers. It was much too big, of course, and she giggled as she pushed it up over her eyes. Robin ran his hand through what remained of his hair. He gave her his biggest, most reassuring smile, and his kindly, rubbery face, slightly sticking-out ears and single little tuft of white hair made her giggle again. He held her dainty, cold hand as gently as he could for fear of crushing it, and then together they took a deep breath and launched themselves into the storm.

He gathered her up in his arms and began to trudge back through the wet sand. It was slow going, first across the sand where they had to stop and brace themselves against waves trying with all their might to pull them away to a watery grave and then on the slippery cobbled road. The moment he set one heavy boot on the stones, he slid forward. Panicked, he flailed about, trying to steady himself, but he still came crashing down painfully on one knee. He set May Bell down, using his massive frame to shield her from the high winds that would have undoubtedly swept her off her feet. Given the number of times he'd fallen on the way to the boat, he worried about injuring her if it happened again. Cracking her head against the stones or having his hefty bulk land on top of her would undoubtedly do her an injury. He shouted in vain to be heard over the growling winds, but she understood nonetheless. She stuck close to him, the whole time hugging his waist—or at least some of it—with one hand, and kept his cap in place on her head with the other. He watched the boiling clouds dash overhead. Rainfall caused the swell to disappear into a murky, misty haze. Waves surged through the sky as clouds gathered on the sea.

"The sea is upside down..." he said, unheard.

May pulled the cap low so it covered her face entirely. Robin knew this meant she wouldn't be able to see anything other than her own feet, but it didn't matter—all she had to do was stay by his side. He tried to cover her with his overcoat, but it made it impossible for her to walk. The weak lantern light was all they had to guide their return, aside from the lightning, and Robin struggled to protect it. They stopped in the same places he had on his way there, catching their breath and steeling themselves for the next leg of the journey. The lights of the Moth & Moon flickered in the distance.

This part would be the hardest, he thought. The open courtyard leading to the door was battered by all manner of flying rubble, from branches and leaves to bits of rope, shingles, and splinters of wood. It was there Robin had slipped the most on his way to find May, and now the winds were even more ferocious. The air was filling with more and more debris, becoming more and more treacherous. He needed something to protect the girl, some way to shield her and himself. It was then he spotted a curved chunk of wood with a piece of rope tied to it. It was being slowly blown across the ground by the high winds. It clattered as it dug into the deep recesses between the cobblestones. From behind the row of sheds, Robin reached out with his long leg and trapped a piece of the rope underfoot. He dragged it towards himself, pulling the wood along with it. It took a few goes to bring it within his grasp, whereupon he hoisted it up and tied it to his arm, reasoning it would make a good shield against the objects whipping through the air. Only after he secured it to his arm did it dawn on him where the wood had come from.

The crimson paint, flaking in places. It was unmistakable. He was using a piece of his dear little boat as a shield. She must have been smashed to pieces in the storm. In a moment of panic, he looked towards the dock, frantically scanning for signs his boat was still afloat. Finding none, he shook his head to put the thought out of his mind and focused on the job at hand. He knew the large surface would make it harder to fight against the wind, but he had no choice. A gust of wind lifted the lantern from his hand and extinguished the flame. They watched as it rattled away into the darkness. They no longer needed it, as there was plenty of light coming from the Moth & Moon. Robin placed May between himself and the shield and together they strode out from behind the shed and into the fray. This was even slower going. The wind tried its best to tear the shield from Robin's arm. It attacked straight on, pulled at it from all sides, pummelled it with stones and branches and slate, but to no avail. He held his course and strode onwards. For one last time, his beloved *Bucca's Call* would protect him from the elements and see him safely home.

They were a few yards from the door when it was swung open by Edwin. Protected, slightly, by the awning around the outside of the building, several men had gathered, holding one another by the arms and forming a human chain out into the storm, calling noiselessly to Robin and his tiny companion as the thunder boomed overhead. Grabbing the sodden sleeve of his overcoat, Edwin gave a signal and the men pulled them all inside, then slammed the door shut behind them. The girl—who was soaking wet and caked with sand—had been too frightened to cry up to that point, but now she ran to her mother and wept. Robin leaned against a wall, relieved as the family reunion took place. May and her mother, Louisa, were by Henry's side now, hugging and tearful and relieved beyond words. Henry's leg was raised on a stool, and he flinched whenever one of the other villagers in the crowded inn accidentally brushed against him.

Robin ached all over. Edwin put his hand on his friend's shoulder and congratulated him. Robin just smiled, and then his eyes rolled back in his head as he sank to the floor, unconscious.

Chapter Seven

WHEN MORWENNA WHITEWATER returned from the privy, she found the crowd abuzz with talk of May Bell's return.

"What have I missed?" she asked a passerby.

Sylvia Farriner pushed her way between the widow and the person she was speaking to and drew herself up to her full height.

"That blundering simpleton you're so fond of brought the girl back, safe and sound."

She was a head taller than Morwenna, but Morwenna wasn't easily intimidated. She looked Sylvia in the eye and adjusted her cane, striking it on the cold floor.

"I knew he'd find her," Morwenna said proudly.

"Well, the girl is safe and sound. Pity the same can't be said for him," Sylvia said as she picked some dirt from beneath her riven fingernails.

Morwenna's bravado faltered and she blinked hard.

"What does that mean? What's happened to him?"

"I'm afraid the strain was too much for the brute's heart, and he collapsed, just over there," Sylvia said, pointing out the exact spot with theatrical relish and mocking concern.

"The men have taken him upstairs," came a raspy voice from behind her.

The tweed golem that was Mrs. Hanniti Kind came to Morwenna's aid, flanked by the substantial form of Mrs. Caddy. Sylvia was well able to take them all on, but it seemed she'd gotten the reaction she had wanted from Morwenna and so she turned and slithered away.

Morwenna shuffled her way upstairs as quickly as her short, dumpy legs and rickety hips would take her, and found Sylvia's son standing outside the closed room door.

"Where is he? Where's Robin?" she demanded.

"He's in there," Edwin replied, "Mr. Bounsell, Mr. Blackwall, and I put him to bed. Doctor Greenaway is in there now, giving him the once-over. He asked me to wait out here."

Morwenna looked at him, sniffed derisively, then marched straight into the room. Dr. Greenaway—a well-dressed, bemonocled man whose enormous bushy grey moustache curled up extravagantly at either end—had pulled the bedclothes down to his patient's waist and was listening to Robin's breathing.

He spluttered and jumped at the intrusion. "I thought I said to wait outside," he said abruptly.

"Giss on! That's all well and good for the local baker, but I should be here. How is he? What's wrong? Robin? Robin, are you awake?" she called as she pushed past the rotund physician.

When she saw the fisherman lying in bed on his back, pale and unmoving, she turned white as a sheet and staggered backwards. For a split second, it seemed as if he was perfectly still, and her heart jumped into her throat. Then his chest rose very slowly and lowered again. Dr. Greenaway hooked his thumbs into his braces, drew himself up to his full height and addressed her.

"Mrs. Whitewater, he's sleeping. He overexerted himself and got a bump on his head when he fell, but he'll be fine. He just needs rest. Lots of rest."

With that, the doctor excused himself and went back downstairs. Morwenna shut the door behind him, much to the surprise of Edwin who had been about to enter. She sat down on the little chair by the bed and fixed the bedclothes back over Robin's broad, smooth chest. She tucked the sheets in, making sure he was nice and warm, and then she fixed what was left of his hair with her hand. She sat there for a time as he slept, thankful it wasn't anything too serious.

"You silly fool," she whispered to him. "You're not as young as you used to be. Why didn't you let someone else go and look for the girl. You could have... You nearly..."

She stopped herself there and straightened her back. Hands resting firmly on her cane, she sniffed the tears away and adjusted her shawl. Then she leaned in close and said, "You're all I have left. Wake up soon, Robin."

There was a knock on the door and she called for it to be opened. Edwin poked his head in and asked if he might enter. Morwenna, in her infinite grace, allowed it.

Edwin started the fire in the hearth on the other side of the room and brought in chairs to hang Robin's wet clothes on.

"You go on back downstairs, Mrs. Whitewater," he said, "I'll stay here and keep an eye on him."

"You don't have to. I'll watch him," Morwenna said.

"No, it's fine. I want to be here, Mrs. Whitewater. He would do the same for me," Edwin replied.

"Very well, but if you're going to stay, it's Morwenna, please."

She studied the baker carefully while the raging winds rattled the shutters. His brow was creased and his green eyes—his mother's eyes—narrowed in concern. They were set a little too far apart for her liking, but they sparkled enough for her to overlook it. All in all, he was quite a good-looking man, she thought, and had an affable face with a square jaw and dimpled chin. His hair was much too short, of course—what kind of man crops it so short you can see his scalp, she wondered. But then it was receding and so she supposed it didn't really matter one way or the other. She remembered him as a child, with a mop of bright, shiny, copper hair. While he might share her hair and eye colour, there wasn't a trace of his mother's spite in him.

After a while sitting in silence, Edwin began to reminisce.

"We've known each other since we were boys," he said. "Though we were never friends when we were young. He was closer to my brother's age, anyway. My parents didn't like Ambrose or me associating with him."

"Hmm, yes, I know. I've had more than one run-in with your mother over the years. She got it into her head that Robin was a bad influence. Afraid he was going to turn out like his father."

"She can be a bit...of a handful," he said, choosing his words carefully. "She has never been an easy person to like, but when Ambrose died, it changed her. Every quirk, every vein of malice, every frayed nerve seemed...amplified, somehow. Exaggerated. Ambrose's wife took their two young sons—my nephews—and moved to Blackrabbit Island. Hester hated my mother. Always did. She couldn't wait to get away from her, always felt like she was trying to... I don't know... control the boys, I suppose? Turn them against their mother. I suppose she's partially the reason why I have to run the bakery alone. Anyway, I'm glad I didn't listen to her. Robin's been a good friend to me in recent years."

"He speaks very highly of you. It's no secret that he doesn't have many friends in this village. He said you were a great help to him after Duncan left," Morwenna said.

She knew Edwin and Robin had become close shortly before Duncan moved to the village, and she began to wonder if perhaps there was more to it than friendship. "Duncan was a nice lad. A bit quiet at times—a bit moody, maybe—but he always treated Robin well."

Duncan might well be thirty-nine years old now, but he'd always be a lad to her.

"Broke his heart when he left. He would hardly talk about him. He'd go out on that boat of his from dawn 'til dusk, wouldn't speak to a soul. It was the same when his dad died. It's a shame he and Duncan couldn't work out their difficulties."

"Do you know what happened between them?" Edwin asked.

Morwenna looked at him somewhat suspiciously. Her little brow furrowed and her eyes became sharper.

"No. Not really. He wouldn't tell me. I assumed you knew?"

Edwin shook his head. "It's odd to see him without his cap, isn't it? Lying there without it, it doesn't even really look like him."

Robin had a big, round face with hooded blue eyes—now closed, of course—and slight, uncoloured lips. His cheeks bore some light scratches from his rescue of May Bell. Double-chinned and bull-necked, he was mostly bald and sprouted only a single little tuft of white hair above his forehead, which his cap normally covered while resting on his small, protruding ears. While some might struggle to describe him as handsome, most everyone would agree he looked gentle, even kind. Despite his size and lumbering stature, he seemed somehow innocent. He smiled a lot; he was good-natured and friendly to everyone. Morwenna always wondered how he managed to be that way. Many people in this town barely tolerated him, all because of his father, and she doubted she could be so magnanimous in that position.

"We have a mutual friend, and we were all in a big group one night at the Moth & Moon and I mentioned I'd never learned to sail," Edwin said.

"Really!" Morwenna exclaimed.

Even she knew her way around a boat. Edwin laughed.

"I know, it's daft. All my life in this village, but I never learned how to sail properly. Someone else had always done it for me, my father usually or my brother. Anyway, Robin offered to take me out in *Bucca's Call* for a few lessons. At first I thought he was just being polite, but he insisted, so a few afternoons that summer, we went out into the bay and he showed me the ropes, taught me the different kind of knots. He was very patient with me. Well, he's patient with everyone, isn't he? Despite how they treat him. I suppose it's something you have to be, to be a fisherman. All that time spent at sea, waiting for fish to bite, or whatever."

"Hmm, yes, but some people can be patient to a fault," Morwenna said.

"True enough. I said to him—I might know my way around an oven and dough, but around ropes and sails, I'm all fingers and thumbs." He laughed gently. "After a few lessons, we found that we got on really well, and that was that, really. When my brother passed away a few months later, Robin was there for me."

"It was very sudden; the whole village was rocked by his passing. It must have been very hard on you," Morwenna said, watching the baker intently. His gaze never left Robin.

"It was. I found myself an only child and in charge of running a whole bakery. My brother, well, he was my rock. He was the dependable, sensible one. Most of the time, anyway. When he was here, I could just, well, I didn't have to grow up, I suppose. I could just let him take care of things. When he was gone, I was so lost, so overwhelmed by everything. I still feel like I'm running to catch up to him. Robin helped me through it all. It's funny how you can know someone your whole life and then one day, you just see them in a whole new light."

"Yes," said Morwenna, "isn't it just."

Chapter Eight

ROBIN AWOKE SEVERAL hours later. The first thing he saw was Edwin sitting on a small chair by the fireplace.

"'ello, Edwin. What 'appened?" Robin asked wearily.

Edwin bolted to his feet. There was an unmistakable look of relief on his face. "You passed out. Too much exertion, I suppose. Once we untied that makeshift shield of yours, we brought you up here. Which wasn't easy, mind, you're even heavier than you look." He laughed softly, nervously. "Doctor Greenaway gave you the once-over. He says you'll be fine. But you need to rest."

Robin smiled. "The girl, is she...?"

"Still upset, but she'll be fine now. Thanks to you."

"Anyone would've done the same."

"I doubt they would've been able to. The wind and rain would have flattened anyone else. Morwenna was here for a while. She had to go back downstairs, but I told her I'd keep an eye on you."

Edwin walked to the window facing the bed and peered out through the shutter slats.

"It's getting worse out there," he said.

The rain pounded mercilessly against the window of the little room, and the shutters bashed and groaned as if they were about to be wrenched from the building. The thunder had grown louder and more frequent. Robin listened to the noise as he carefully sat himself up. He rubbed his arm where the rope had been tied. It still throbbed a little. The room was much like the other bedrooms in the tavern—unpainted, with bare floorboards, a tiny wardrobe, and a simple bed. The small fire flickering in the cast-iron grate was enough to warm the room. In front of it, his clothes and a towel were draped over a couple of wicker chairs. His garments had been completely drenched but were drying nicely.

Edwin rubbed his freckled hand over his own short-cropped hair and onto the back of his neck, and walked over to the edge of the bed.

"You look terrible," Robin observed.

"Thanks a bunch." Edwin laughed.

"What I mean is—you look tired. And it's not because of what 'appened to me. You're runnin' yourself ragged," Robin said, his voice husky and dry.

"Leave it, Robin. It's not me who needs to rest right now. It's you." Edwin hesitated and took a deep breath as the thunder boomed overhead. "When you slid down the wall, I thought we'd lost you."

He paused then, his eyes becoming glassy and red.

"I'll be fine, Edwin," Robin said and took his friend by the hand. "Don't you worry. Take more 'n that to finish me off." he said, laughing.

Edwin smiled and pointed to a glass of whiskey next to a big brass bell on the bedside table. "Mr. Reed thought you might need something to help get you going," Edwin said of the drink. "And he thought the bell would be handy if you needed to get attention. Just ring it; I'll come running."

"Assumin' you'll hear it over the noise of the storm and that lot downstairs!" Robin chortled.

The rabble in the tavern was becoming as clamorous as the storm outside. The people of the village were making the most of their unexpected captivity.

"Don't worry; I'll be listening out for it," Edwin said from the doorway. "I'll check in on you in a couple of hours."

"You don't need to," Robin said, not wanting to cause a fuss.

"Yes, I do." Edwin smiled.

Robin watched him leave. He lay there for a time, grateful for the rest. The fire was comforting and the blankets were heavy and warm. He decided to let his clothes dry some more, and as he listened to rain pounding the shutters, he thought about that look in Edwin's eyes. The relief in them. It cheered him greatly to know his friend cared so deeply for him. As they had grown close in recent years, there were times when Robin wondered if their closeness would blossom into something more, but he knew it couldn't happen. The risk of ruining what they had—a true friendship, for probably the first time for either of them. Was it really worth the gamble? Besides, Edwin didn't think of him that way, he reasoned. Robin doubted Edwin thought of anyone that way. As far as he could tell, Edwin spent almost every waking hour either in the bakery or worrying about it, leaving little time for anything else.

Still, Robin closed his eyes, put his hands behind his head, and allowed himself the luxury of musing on what it might be like if Edwin were amenable to a closer relationship. What he might say if he thought Edwin would listen. But there it was again—that old, familiar feeling, the weight on his heart, the knot in his stomach. The knot made of every mistake he'd ever made, every stupid thing he'd ever said, everything he should have done, everything he missed, everything he let go of when he should have fought for it—each one a thread in his knot. He closed his eyes as his blood pounded in his ears, louder even than the storm outside. He hadn't the strength to force it away this time, to shove it down back into the little black box in his soul where it belonged. There was one thread in this knot far larger than the rest.

Duncan.

Always there when he tried to sleep, always there when he felt weak, when he felt tired. Only at sea did he find respite, only on the waves, only on *Bucca's Call*. There was a new thread in his knot now—his boat, his haven, gone. The enormity of it was too much for him to accept. His thoughts drifted back to that morning, meeting Duncan on his way home. The knot tightened sharply and in his weakened state, something inside snapped, something in his mind fractured. His whole body began to shake violently; he felt dizzy, like he might vomit, sweat gathered on his brow as he covered his face with his trembling hands, and he knew then, finally, that he couldn't ignore it any longer. He could wait no more—he had to speak to Duncan, had to explain himself, explain his actions. Worse—his inactions. He knew then and there that if he didn't, the knot would never untangle.

He thought also about Edwin and Morwenna sitting at his bedside, watching over him. He thought about Dr. Greenaway tending to him. What if the doctor hadn't been there? What if he had pushed himself just a little further? Maybe he wouldn't be lying there, thinking about his mistakes. The thought made his heart pound harder. He thought of all the things he'd left unsaid, all the mistakes that wouldn't die with him but would live on in the hearts and minds of others, growing and festering, never to be fixed. That thought scared him more than he could ever have expected. And so as he lay there, listening to the hurricane and the music and laughter from the bar below, he resolved to finally, finally take action. First and most importantly, he had to set things right with Duncan. It was the key to everything for him. It might not work—he felt like Duncan would never, could never, forgive him—but he had to at least try. He couldn't rush this. It would take time to work out what he would say or he could end up hurting Duncan even more. Soon, he drifted into sleep, and as he'd made up his mind to make amends, he felt the knot loosen, just a little.

Edwin began to make his way downstairs but stopped, putting his hand on the rail. He spotted an open door to an empty bedroom and quickly ducked inside, closed the door and rested his back against it. The room had been prepared with fresh bedding, kindling for the fire, and water in a large, ceramic jug.

He began shaking uncontrollably. Wobbling across the room, he sat on the bed, held his sinewy hands up as they quivered, then let out something between a laugh and a sob. All the stress and anxiety of the past few hours—of the past few years, if he was being honest—came pouring out of him. It was as though the floodgates in his mind had opened. He'd buried so much for so long, and now it had all come gushing to the surface. He couldn't stop himself from thinking about what would have happened if Robin had died. Tears streamed down his face as he gently rocked back and forth where he sat. He covered his mouth to stifle any further outbursts and sat for a while, feeling the most exquisite relief.

When he felt back under control, he poured some water from the jug into a bowl, lifted a cloth, and washed his face. His eyes were still bloodshot, but in the dim lantern light of the inn, he reasoned no one would notice. Or care. He wrung out the cloth, smoothed out the bedsheets, and left the room as he had found it.

Downstairs, Ladies Eva and Iris Wolfe-Chase stood making small-talk by the bar. They were quite the most well-dressed of the village women, always smartly turned out in flowing dresses of vivid hues and the most splendid lace. Eva was statuesque. Carved from ice, she was slim and sharp-featured, with raven hair tied back in a bun. Her wife, Iris, was petite with wide, friendly eyes, a perpetually smiling rosebud mouth, and copper hair that burned in wide, fiery curls as it tumbled about her shoulders.

Eva had been raised in a splendid country house on Blackrabbit Island, which lay north of Merryapple—between it and mainland. Her family was the wealthiest in the area. After their passionate and torrid courtship—and their whirlwind handfasting—it had taken some convincing for Eva to come live in this sleepy village instead of moving to a large city on the mainland, but this was where Iris had been born and raised, and she simply couldn't imagine wanting to live anywhere else. The Chase family owned some of the ships that used the cove, and Eva soon found living there made it easier to deal with the captains. She had only moved to the island within the past year, and was still settling in and exploring all the nooks and crannies of village life. She had expected to find the place a trifle stifling, but she had been welcomed with open arms by the community. Iris had always been well-liked, and the whole village rejoiced in her happiness with her new bride. An unexpected benefit of living there meant that through her direct dealings with the various captains employed by the Chase Trading Company, Eva had her pick of the clothing imported from all four corners of the globe, ensuring she was the best dressed woman on any of the islands.

The Wolfe clan weren't short of a bob or two, either. They had been blacksmiths for generations, but Iris, with her dainty wrists and slim arms, wasn't exactly suited to carrying on the family business and so she left it to her uncle and his sons, who were camped somewhere on the second floor of the inn, having found a comfortable antechamber buried deep within the arcane architecture of the tavern. Their forge was situated between Anchor Rise and Hill Road, and had been built around the same time as the Moth & Moon. All of the metalwork used there, and in the rest of the village, came from that solitary forge.

Eva noticed Edwin descending the staircase and called him over, presenting him with a tankard of scrumpy.

"Ladies!" Edwin exclaimed. "How lovely. I wasn't sure if you'd be here. I thought Wolfe-Chase Lodge more than capable of resisting a little rain?"

They were frequent customers at his bakery, usually ordering some outlandish dessert for one of their many dinner parties, several of which he had attended. He bent down to kiss Iris on the cheek, then leaned in to do the same to Eva, for she was as tall as he was. Their house had been in the Wolfe family for generations and was the largest in the village. Anchor Rise had grown up around it, as the homes there were originally built to house the staff members needed to run the residence.

"We wouldn't dream of missing out on a gathering like this." Iris smiled.

"Although it's a shame we couldn't have gathered somewhere a bit less...fragrant," Eva said, ostentatiously covering her smile with a delicate handkerchief. She fondled the lapel of Edwin's borrowed mushroom coat and made a friendly disapproving tut. She was dressed in a stunning purple redingote with teal and gold accents, which tapered in at her waspish waist. Iris was more modestly clad in a sequined and embroidered silk dress, patterned with tiny daisies. Both women went bonnetless.

"Oh stop, it's not that bad here." Iris laughed, poking Eva in the ribs.

A small girl ran past, pushing her way between the two women, giggling like a loon. She was followed by two more children, who scampered around them. Eva cocked an eyebrow in Edwin's direction, who laughed.

Eva had never really liked the Moth & Moon. It was considerably too public for her refined tastes or so she would have everyone believe. Secretly, she enjoyed the chance to eavesdrop on the latest village gossip, though she wished it could be done in a more luxurious locale.

"I'm sure we could find a quieter spot for you both," Edwin said, but Iris scoffed at the notion.

"Oh no," she said, "I like it here. Lots to keep one's mind and eye occupied!"

"How are you, Mr. Farriner?" Eva asked, trying to take her mind off her surroundings. "Are your parents here?"

"They decided to wait the storm out at home..." Edwin began.

"Ah," Eva interrupted. "Shame." She shared a sly look with Iris who poked her gently in the ribs once again. Edwin was oblivious to this.

"...but they arrived some time ago. I think they're out in one of the back rooms somewhere. I suppose the weather got too bad for them to stay at home."

"Oh. Well. Good." Eva turned slightly and took a long, empathic sip from her drink.

"We heard the excitement earlier. I trust Mr. Shipp is well?" Iris asked sweetly.

"Yes, yes, as well as can be expected, I suppose. He's awake and recuperating upstairs."

"You must have gotten quite a fright, seeing him collapse," Eva said, watching from behind her handkerchief and studying Edwin's reaction. She had noticed the redness in his eyes straight away and deduced the reason. Iris shot her another knowing look.

"I did," he said, taking a swig of cider. "Near stopped my heart, to be honest. I thought I'd...thought we'd lost him."

Iris stroked his arm. "You poor thing."

"Seeing him lying there, it just...it brought a lot of memories back." He frowned.

Eva was surprised by the baker's candour and cocked a curious eyebrow. Edwin wasn't secretive by any means, but nor was he usually so forthcoming with his feelings.

"You stayed up there with him, by his bedside, until he woke?" Iris angled.

"Someone had to." Edwin shrugged, blushing a bit. "I'm sure he'd have preferred if Duncan was there, but wouldn't be safe leaving him alone. Wouldn't be right, either—him waking up with no one there."

"Quite," Eva and Iris said in unison.

Chapter Nine

A LITTLE WHILE later, Robin dressed, left the room on the upper floor, and carefully picked his way downstairs. His clothes were still warm and toasty from the fire and reminded him of when he was a boy and his father would warm his clothes for him before he got up on cold winter mornings. On his way down the many staircases dotted disjointedly around the structure, he spotted Mr. Reed hanging over the railings on the second-floor gallery, holding a lantern up to the darkest recesses of the timberwork with one hand, and grasping a small stick tipped with a net in the other. The short innkeeper was balanced rather precariously on his little round stomach while a tough, scarred, and tattooed pilchard fisherman named Mr. Penny held him steady by grabbing the belt around his waist. The fisherman laughed with his companions, pretending to let go of the belt on more than one occasion. Robin wondered what could possibly be so important as to require such extraordinary gymnastics.

"I'm sure I saw something here," Mr. Reed said.

On the ground floor, May Bell saw Robin descend the final staircase and rushed over to him. She gave him a big hug and put his cap back on his head. This, too, had been dried—albeit by the large fireplace on the ground floor—and it was toasty and comforting on his head. He had felt quite naked without it, and with it back in its rightful place, he was whole once again.

Morwenna was still reigning by the fireplace, though she was quieter than normal. She perked up when she spotted Robin lumbering through the crowd, causing more than one spillage from a bumped tankard. Even though he slouched, he was still much taller than most other people in the village.

"Robin!" she called as he stooped down to hug her. She held his big face in her hands for a moment and began to well up. "Edwin should have told me you were awake. I'd have come up to see you, but I thought you'd be resting. Should you be up and about so soon?"

"I'm fine, Morwenner," he said.

She just smiled and said, "Can we talk later?"

"Later," Robin nodded. "I promise."

To his immense surprise, he was being congratulated by almost every one of the elder women forming the knights of Morwenna Whitewater's round table. Given how this marked a significant change from how they usually reacted to him, he was quite unsure of how to react. He thanked them awkwardly, thrust his hands into the pockets of his breeches, and squeezed his shoulders together, thoroughly uncomfortable with their appreciation, though he tried not to show it. He failed, of course, but he did try really, really hard.

The air had become thick with the acrid smoke of the many pipes peppering the crowd. Every now and then, a sunset-red haze flared in the little clay pots. He spotted Edwin across the packed room and began to make his way over to him. He was stopped many times by grateful villagers who heard of his brave rescue and took the opportunity to shake his hand and slap him on his back. The handshakes were appreciated, but the back slaps made him wince a little.

At the bar, Eva and Iris Wolfe-Chase greeted him and said how glad they were to see him back on his feet. Mr. Reed, having dismounted from the railings and made his way back behind the bar—through what Robin could only assume was some secret, possibly magical set of stairs—handed over another small glass of whiskey to him.

"For the big hero," he said.

He actually meant it, but his tone and dour demeanour would suggest otherwise to those who didn't really know him. George Reed was one of the few people in the village who Robin felt close to. They had spent the occasional evening deep in conversation together, long after the drinkers had left to stagger up the cobbled streets of Blashy Cove, singing at the tops of their voices. He knew Mr. Reed had occasionally stuck up for him when others ran him down, even though he had told him many times there was no need. Robin thanked him for the drink and considered mentioning how he was almost positive he'd snapped a wooden slat in the bed while getting out of it. He was honest to a fault, but he didn't want to spoil the mood or add to the innkeeper's worries. Anyway, it was probably fine, he thought.

He slid around the table and into the booth as gently as he could, which meant only knocking over one drink instead of all of them.

"Ladies Wolfe-Chase," he said, doffing his cap.

"We're going to be here all night and I can't be doing with Lady this and Lady that the whole time. I'm Eva, this is Iris. Let's save the formalities for another day, please."

"If you insist!" Robin said, laughing.

Once he was settled and relaxed, Eva slipped one slender arm under his beefy, bejumpered bicep.

"You know, Robin," she said in a silky tone of voice, "I can call you Robin, can't I? You were unconscious for a long time, and Edwin here never left your side for a moment."

"Really?" he said, beaming. He turned to Edwin who was blushing.

"Well," he coughed, as his ears turned so red they looked as though they might burn through his skull, "someone had to do it."

Eva leaned in even closer and whispered to Robin. "He'd have waited there all night if you'd needed him to."

People were swirling around the whole tavern in eddying waves, with new little enclaves forming every few minutes. A group from a nearby booth moved on, and Robin and his companions took it over. Eva suggested they move somewhere more private when the opportunity arose, as the booth was very much at the centre of the action. Iris, however, said she was happy to stay put and everyone knew that meant they would be going nowhere. They all sat and watched Mr. Reed who was now frantically running around the ground floor, grumpily making sure everyone had what they needed. Running the Moth & Moon was a massive undertaking. Mr. Reed had a small company of men and women in his employ who acted as waiters, bartenders, cleaners, chambermaids, cooks, carpenters, painters, and everything in between. He was back behind the bar now, in his favourite spot. Behind him on the wall was a brass trumpet, a mask made from silver and grey pigeon feathers, and a large, glass-fronted box in which were pinned a variety of moth types found on the island. The centrepiece was a huge, pale, female emperor moth, her wings spread wide and patterned with what looked like swirling, looping eyes, watching over the innkeeper and his premises.

"I don't know why he doesn't just sell the place," said Edwin. "He obviously doesn't want to run it."

"Who'd buy it?" laughed Robin.

"Well, my father, for one," said Eva.

Iris looked surprised. "Really?"

"Oh, yes. He offered to buy it when Mr. Reed's parents died and several times before then, come to think of it. He thought it would be a good investment."

"And if there's one thing Marley Chase knows, it's a good investment." Iris smiled. "Oh! Just think, if he had bought it, he might have raised you here, instead of at Chase Manor! You could have been a bar girl!"

"Hardly," Eva scoffed. "I'd have spilled a few too many drinks on purpose, that would have put him off the idea. You know how father hates waste. What about your parents, Edwin? Your father was a baker as well, wasn't he?"

"Oh yes, his mother was an excellent cook, taught him all she knew. We still use her recipes today, in fact. He worked in the kitchens here at the inn for a while. Learned his trade. But he got fed up of not getting the credit for his hard work, so he opened the bakery. He'd still be working there if Mum didn't make him stay at home."

"He's earned his retirement. He should enjoy it," Eva said. "A life of leisure, I quite envy him."

Robin thought she wasn't far off living one herself. What little work she did do involved cracking the whip at lazy Chase Trading Company captains, and he'd seen how she relished it. He often thought she'd have used an actual whip if she thought she could get away with it.

"But you really should take on someone to help you at the bakery. It's entirely too much work for one man." Eva said.

Edwin shifted about uncomfortably in his seat. "I don't need anyone," he said defensively. His head sank and he fixed his eyes squarely on his tankard. "I can manage."

Iris smiled warmly at him. "Edwin, it's not that we think you can't cope, but it's a lot for one person to take on. Without your brother or father, you're doing to work of three men."

"Ambrose managed it for long enough. So can I. I wasn't much help to him when he was alive, and Dad hasn't been right for years. Much as he complains, he's better off out of it. It's hard for a man who's worked all his life to just sit back and do nothing, but his hands don't work like they used to," Edwin said.

One night while drunk, Edwin had confessed to Robin he was worried about the same thing happening to his own hands. He was in his early forties and found his joints were already becoming stiffer, and without a child to carry on in his name—or his nephews to pass the bakery to—Edwin wondered what would happen to him and the bakery when he was no longer able to work. Robin hadn't had any answers for him.

There was a heavy silence. Robin felt they'd pushed him too far, invaded too much and now struggled to think of what to say. It was then that May Bell bounced over to their table.

"Hullo, Mr. Farriner!" she called cheerfully.

Edwin sat up and smiled back.

"Is there anything you need?" May asked. "Anything I can get for you?"

"No, I think I'm fine, thank you, May. I hope this rain doesn't last too long, or there'll be no bread for you to deliver tomorrow!" Edwin said as pleasantly as he could manage.

Even Robin noticed how careful Edwin always was to speak to children in as friendly a manner as he could muster. He knew it was because of how Edwin's mother had treated him when he was a boy, always making him feel like he was a nuisance.

"If you need me to help clean up the bakery after the storm, just say so," May said and bounded off again in the direction of some children her own age.

Eva slinked over beside Edwin and slipped her arm around his.

"You know," she said seductively, and just a little louder than before, "if you did take on some help—say, an apprentice—you'd have someone to assist you in the bakery, and you'd also have more time for...*other* pursuits."

She let that sink in and before Edwin had a chance to respond she unlocked herself from his arm and turned to face Robin.

"Now, Robin," she said regally. "We've never had a chance to properly talk, and it looks like we may not get a better time, since it seems as though this entire island is about to be blown away overnight."

As if in direct response to this, the whole inn shook with the tremendous force of the hurricane winds and a terrific flare of lightning illuminated the battered shutters.

"I've heard lots of stories about you and your father. I'm sure you won't be surprised to hear several of our mutual neighbours warned me about you but true to maddening island form, refused to elaborate on why. Whatever have you done to earn such notoriety?"

It was Robin's turn to shift about uncomfortably in his seat. Edwin did it again too, in sympathy. Iris just buried her face in her hands.

"You 'aven't 'eard about Captain Erasmus Shipp?" Robin said, getting himself settled. With his thick accent, it always sounded like he was adding far too much emphasis on the *a* in 'Erasmus.' It was drawn out, like a wall to be climbed before he could reach the end of his father's name.

Eva coughed slightly. "Well, I've heard stories, of course. Rumours, to be more accurate."

"Oh yes, I'm sure I know exactly what rumours you've 'eard," he said. "It's not an 'appy tale. Not entirely. You sure you want to 'ear it?"

The two women nodded enthusiastically.

"It all started one mornin', back along when all the fishermen of the village were headin' to the dock, gettin' ready for the day's work. One of 'em hears cryin' comin' from one of the boats and calls the others round to 'ave a look, you see. They lift up an old oilskin tarp and there, swaddled in some old rags, is an infant, barely a day old. My dad, Erasmus, well 'e lifts the baby out and sees a note pinned to 'im."

"Pinned to the baby?!" Iris cried.

"Pinned to the swaddling, dear," her wife corrected, with a look of playful derision.

"Oh, yes. Of course. Do go on, Robin."

"Anyway, this note says Erasmus were the baby's father, and 'is mother were a woman named Rose, who 'e 'ad met on Blackrabbit Island. About nine months earlier, presumably. The note said she couldn't look after the baby, and she 'oped Erasmus would. The note also said the baby's name were Robin."

He took a sip of whiskey while he let the moment land. Eva and Iris were both a little bewildered and sat gaping like freshly caught pilchards on a sun-baked deck.

"Tell them the best bit," Edwin said. He'd heard the story a few times before.

"Guess which boat they found me in." Robin smiled.

"You're joking," Eva replied. Working with the sailors meant she knew every boat and captain in the port.

"Nope." Robin laughed.

"Which one?" her wife asked, a little behind.

"*Bucca's Call*," she said. "They found you, as an infant, on board your own boat?"

"Yup." He laughed again. A deep, bellowing, hearty laugh.

"Oh, you're having us on. This is like when my mother told me I was found in a cabbage patch," Eva said, turning her back towards Robin in exaggerated admonishment.

Robin held his mammoth hands up, still chuckling. "I swear on me life, it's all true. You can ask Mrs. Whitewater. She were there, saw the whole thing. Even Edwin's parents were there. Most of the town came out to see what all the fuss were about. *Bucca's Call* belonged to my dad first. 'E were well known as a bit of a ladies man. 'E toured the islands in 'er. This Rose woman must 'ave come to Merryapple in the middle of the night, recognised Dad's boat, and left me in 'er for 'im to find. Probably a better prospect than knockin' on every door in town tryin' to find 'im."

"That's...that's astonishing. And what about Rose? Did you ever hear from her again?" Iris asked, eyes wide with curiosity.

"No, never." Robin paused there for a moment. "I went to Blackrabbit a few times, tryin' to find 'er. There are a few women named Rose there, but none of them were the right age. She must have left soon after I was born. Or died, I suppose. That 'appens to women, doesn't it? Sometimes, after childbirth? Complications and that? She were in a boat, probably on 'er own. Maybe somethin' 'appened to 'er on the way back to Blackrabbit. I asked around, travelled to all of the towns, but nobody knew who she were. It's a funny feelin', not knowin' for sure if you're an orphan or not," he said with a forced smile.

"I can't believe we've never heard this story before," Eva said. "We need to invite you round for dinner some evening, Mr. Shipp. I had no idea you were shrouded in such mystery!"

"Well, thank you kindly," Robin replied, doffing his cap.

"So, what happened to your father?" Iris asked.

"Ah, right, I were comin' to that. One night, when I were about ten, 'e apparently signed on to a whaling vessel docked out in the cove and I never saw 'im again. No farewells or nothin', he just left a will on the kitchen table—one line he wrote in an 'urry, with a signature. 'I, Erasmus Shipp, do 'ereby bequeath all my worldly belongin's to my son, Robin Jonas Shipp.' And that were that. 'E just left. A couple of days later, we got word the ship 'ad sank, with all souls on board lost. Now, the bit you've probably been told is the night he left were the same night Mrs. Whitewater's 'usband, Barnabas, died."

His thick accent stumbled over the *ar* this time.

"They found 'im on the rocks around the southeast of the island. 'E must have slipped from the 'eadland. At least, that's what Mrs. Whitewater says 'appened. There were talk, though, that my dad were to blame."

"Surely not!" Iris exclaimed.

"Well, folk at the time thought it were 'ighly suspicious that Barnabas died the same night Erasmus left. And once they found out 'e'd left a will, well, as far as they were concerned, 'e were guilty. 'E'd murdered Barnabas and run away. But then when we got word about the ship sinkin', that sort of put the matter to bed, really. Nothin' more to be done."

"Oh, I'm terribly sorry," Iris said, reaching out and putting her tiny porcelain hand on Robin's massive, coarse fist. He smiled at the tiny, flame-haired woman next to him.

"I don't believe 'e 'ad anything to do with Barnabas's death. Neither does Mrs. Whitewater. They were all friends. But some people round 'ere just won't be told." He glanced over in the direction of Mrs. Greenaway, who was deep in the heart of Morwenna Whitewater's coterie. "I spent almost as much time with Barnabas as I did with Dad. Barnabas even painted that portrait of 'im on my landin'."

Edwin nodded at this. He'd been to Robin's house a few times and seen the painting looming down from the landing.

"Dad could be sullen and a bit moody at times, but 'e weren't no killer. Me and 'im used to spend 'ours out in the cove. 'E taught me 'ow to sail. 'ow to fish. I remember the day I landed my first pilchard. 'E were so proud 'e couldn't stop smilin'."

Robin straightened his hat, fixing the visor so it was centred over his eyes.

"'E took this cap off 'is 'ead and put it on me. It were too big, at first, but I soon grew into it." he said with a chuckle. "Before 'e left, 'e made sure I were looked after, left me Bucca, the 'ouse, the money. I suppose 'e must have known 'e weren't coming back even if the ship 'adn't sank. Ever since then, the people of the village 'ave eyed me a bit suspiciously, like the apple 'asn't fallen far from the tree, I suppose."

The smile was gone now, replaced with a sadness many years in the making. It had been a long time, but he still missed his father. Still felt abandoned.

"'E used to 'ave this journal that 'e wrote in all the time. Brought it everywhere with 'im, 'e did. A little blood-red book 'e got on 'is first voyage at sea. Sometimes I wish I 'ad it. I wonder if 'e wrote about what 'appened, why 'e left. When I think about what must be in it—'is life, 'is voyages, 'is time spent at sea with Grandad..."

"What happened to it?" Iris asked.

"'E took it with 'im when 'e left. All that 'istory, lost with 'im. It's a shame. Sometimes, I imagine findin' it washed up onshore in a bottle. Like maybe 'e'd put it in one and thrown it overboard before the boat sank. Somehow, it'd find its way 'ere. Silly, really."

Robin thought about telling them what had happened earlier, how his boat was either lying in pieces on the beach or sunk in the cove, but winced at the very idea and found the words too difficult to say. Remembering he was in company, he sought to liven the mood.

"The randy goat probably ran off with some woman. Mrs. Caddy says she's amazed there weren't more babies left in 'is boat!"

Despite the hurricane battering their tiny island, spirits were raised and the villagers had settled in for the night. There had been a few minor scuffles at first, some toes trodden on—both figuratively and literally—while everyone adjusted to the situation, but they had mostly died down.

A few men had pulled out their fiddles and struck up a tune, someone else produced a type of drum known as a crowdy-crawn, and another a set of pipes. While people had been playing instruments in random isolation throughout the day, now a proper music session had begun and some of the sailors had gathered to sing some shanties. Mrs. Louisa Bell turned out to have a strikingly beautiful singing voice. She sang an old song her grandmother had taught her about a woman standing by a gnarled tree on a cliff, waiting for her husband to return home from sea. It was only afterward she'd realised how this probably hadn't been a good idea, given how Mrs. Stillpond was worried sick about her husband and son still being out in the storm. Some of the other musicians picked up on this as well and changed the tempo considerably, allowing Mr. Penny a chance to sing a rather bawdy song about two pirates, a barrel of rum and a tropical island boy.

It was getting late, and people were handing out blankets to those who hadn't thought to bring any. The rooms upstairs were filled with the elderly and infirm of the village. A handful of residents had suffered minor injuries as a result of the high winds. Everyone else had to make do with whatever space they could find. Sylvia Farriner had tried to intimidate one elderly man out of his bed on an upper floor, but Nathaniel, fearing she was up to something, had followed her and dragged her away, apologising to the gentleman as he did so. He got her settled on a cushioned bench at the back of the tavern, while he sat on a couple of wobbly stools, wrapped an old blanket around his shoulders, and propped himself up against a knobbled wall.

Some villagers settled into large chairs whose leather had become cracked and worn through years of use and misuse. Others stretched out on padded benches, or across tables. A few hardy souls resolved to lie on the cold floors, which necessitated many extra blankets. Although some had already fallen asleep, there was still a hum of chatter and laughter from most of the occupants.

At the back of the tavern, in some anterooms set aside for younger inhabitants, mothers were settling their children and assuring them that everything would be better in the morning.

Chapter Ten

IN THE LITTLE blue house on the hill, Duncan was attempting to read a book by the fire. He never seemed to get more than a couple of sentences read before his mind wandered back to his meeting with Robin earlier in the day. In spite of himself, he was uneasy. He kept telling himself the Moth & Moon was the safest place to be, but every peal of thunder and snapping tree branch filled his mind with worries.

Slamming the book shut, he got up from his velvet armchair. Peering through the shutters, something odd caught Duncan's eye—through the miasma of the hurricane, he could just see a blinking light in one of the west-facing windows of the lighthouse. It was a repeating pattern. Three blinks, then a pause, then three again. Someone was in distress. From the angle, he knew no one in the Moth & Moon would have been able to see it. A mild dread began to grip him. He knew there were two attendants in the lighthouse—Keeper Knott and Keeper Hall. The main lamp was still radiating its brilliant beam out to sea, but something must have happened to one or both of the keepers.

Duncan frantically paced up and down the room for a few moments. There was nothing else for it—he'd have to go to the lighthouse. There wasn't anyone else. Taking a deep breath, he pulled on his heaviest boots and tricorne cap, then his midnight-blue overcoat. The fine gold thread caught the light from the fire and glinted as it wove around in surprisingly delicate patterns.

Outside, he clutched his cap tightly and began the journey down the steep roads towards the harbour. He thought the winds had begun to ease a little and was grateful for the small mercy, but then he noticed the rain had stopped entirely. Pausing in his tracks, he turned his head to the sky. Heavy grey clouds remained overhead, but now there was scarcely a breeze.

"The eye of the hurricane," he mumbled to himself.

He hurried down the pathway from his house on the hill, down to the laneway to the coast. It was eerily quiet and still after the clamour of the storm. He paused for a moment, surveying the damage already done. Downed trees, loosened slate tiles, and scattered thatch littered the village. Just then, he became aware of a faint sound, barely a whisper above the sound of the still-rough sea. He pretended not to notice and carried on a few steps before hearing it again. A pathetic, desperate bawling. He closed his eyes, hoping it would stop. He didn't have time for this, but on and on, it went. He knew what it was. In an instant, he'd been flung back to his childhood, lying in bed, awakened by a storm and a similar cry, one he ignored, angered at having being roused from sleep. The following morning he'd found the source—one of the recent litter from the farm's cat had crawled from its bedding and trapped its neck between a box and the barn wall. Its body hung lifeless, mouth still open. The image of that had haunted him for years. He couldn't shake the thought of the tiny, forlorn creature crying for help, and how he'd ignored it. He could have saved it if he'd just gotten out of bed. He remembered how callous and unconcerned his father had been when he'd told him over breakfast of the creature's plight.

"Just an animal," his father had said, taking another bite of bread. "Just an animal."

"Damn it," Duncan said, turning back towards the source of the noise.

It was coming from the hedgerow beside him. He'd often stopped and picked blackberries from it on his way past. The faint moonlight barely illuminated the clouds overhead, so he held his lantern close. After some searching, he found the source of the noise—a tiny black and white kitten. Not days old, but not yet months either. Its bright blue eyes threw back the lantern light, and its mewling grew louder when it noticed Duncan.

"What's all the noise about? Where's your mother?" Duncan asked, searching through the bramble. In short order, he found her and the rest of the litter. All dead. They'd been crushed and buried by shingles blown loose by the winds.

Sighing heavily—resigned to the obvious course of action—he reached in through the dripping wet blackberry bushes and carefully lifted the kitten to his chest. The tiny creature meowed in protest, as loudly as its feeble lungs could manage.

"Shut up, you little idiot, I'm trying to help you," Duncan tutted.

He examined the kitten for any injuries but found none. He did notice, however, that one of its front legs was a little shorter than the other. He wrapped the kitten into the safety of his coat and wondered what to do next. There was no time to bring the animal back to his home—the people in the lighthouse needed him. He couldn't just leave it there, either. He knew what his father would do, but Duncan could never be quite so heartless. He hesitated for a heartbeat before throwing his head back and yelling at the sky.

"Fine, you're coming with me. Maybe someone at the inn will take you off my hands."

Chapter Eleven

IN THE MOTH & Moon, it took a few minutes for the villagers to notice the winds had stopped. Cautiously, some people began to peer out of the windows and even prepared to venture outside. The younger folk, most of whom had been entirely too excited to sleep, began to cheer, thinking it was over, but the elders knew it was just the eye of the storm and warned them to stay indoors. The calm centre of a hurricane could last for minutes or days; there was no way to tell. That's what made them so dangerous.

Robin and his companions hadn't found anywhere to lie down for the night, so they had nestled in the corners of their alcove, closed their eyes, and tried to get some rest. Edwin was wrapped up in his father's coat and dozing peacefully. Iris was lying with her head resting against his heavy arm and twitched slightly as she slept. Eva was wide awake, as was Robin. She couldn't sleep unless it was in a comfortable bed in a quiet room, and Robin had slept enough earlier on. They occasionally spoke in hushed whispers, but for the most part, each was lost in thought.

They became aware of the commotion happening at the entrance across the bar and leaned out from their alcove to get a better look. News of the break in the weather was rippling through the crowd. The noise woke Edwin and, in turn, Iris, who sat up, yawned, and stretched.

"Oh!" she said suddenly. "I've just had a rather brilliant thought. Robin, Eva's family has owned a lot of boats that use Blashy Cove, perhaps she might be able to find out what happened to the ship your father disappeared on."

"That's a good idea," said Edwin. "I never thought of that."

"Do you happen to know the name of it?" Iris asked.

"It were named the *Caldera*. I tried to find out exactly what 'appened to 'er a few times over the years, but nobody knew."

Even Robin noticed the look of shock on Eva's face.

"What? You've 'eard of 'er?" he asked hopefully.

Eva looked to Iris, then to Edwin. She picked up a glass of whiskey that had been sitting unmolested on their table for some time

"That ship, the *Caldera*. I know it well. It was indeed one of my family's vessels." She cleared her throat again. "I'm aware the natives of Merryapple enjoy beating around the bush, but that's simply not in my nature, so what I say now I say with kindness, though it may sound otherwise. Mr. Shipp, the *Caldera* was a pirate vessel."

Robin looked as if he'd been slapped in the face.

"My father was initially unaware of this, but he discovered its captain, one Thomas Oughterlauney, was using it—a Chase Trading Company vessel—to attack and sink other ships. Father had hired the man in good faith, but then rumours about his past began to surface. My father had a number of investigators in his organisation, and he tasked one with compiling a report on Oughterlauney's life—a report that was buried in the company files. It contains every detail the investigator could dig up. Details of Oughterlauney's piracy. My father was not pleased to discover that he had sunk one of the company's craft years earlier, in 1726. Here, as a matter of fact, in the cove, when Oughterlauney was planning to attack this village but was thwarted by an alliance between my father's ships and one other."

"I've heard my mum and dad talk about that. It was quite a battle, by all accounts," Edwin said.

"In 1740, I believe it was, my father quietly dispatched two vessels to capture or sink the *Caldera*. They received word that Captain Oughterlauney's ship had been sighted off the coast of Merryapple but didn't seem to be acting aggressively. Fearing the village might be damaged should they engage in combat, they chose to wait until the pirates were in the waters between here and Blackrabbit Island before attacking."

Eva cleared her throat one more time, her voice faltering.

"Oughterlauney was unprepared for battle, and the *Caldera* was sunk. All hands were lost. Mr. Shipp, I'm afraid it seems my father was ultimately responsible for your father's death."

She quivered slightly as she downed the entire glass of whiskey in her hand. Robin sat back into the cushioned alcove and slowly tugged on his earlobe.

"Are you sure about this?" he asked quietly.

Eva nodded. "I recognise the name. I'm very familiar with my family business's entire history. It was the only way I could be taken seriously by the captains I deal with every day. I had to know more than they did. I had to know everything, including information my father didn't make public. He was afraid word of the *Caldera*'s activities would get out, that it would make his company look bad, make *him* look bad for not knowing about it sooner, so he made sure it was kept quiet. He paid off the crews of the ships that sank it and buried all the records. I found them years ago in his study. I memorised them. Did you know? That your father was involved in piracy?" she asked brusquely.

"No. No, I didn't," said Robin. "Thank you for tellin' me this, Lady Wolfe-Chase."

Suddenly, the heavy oak doors of the inn were flung wide open with a loud bang as Duncan burst in, panting and somewhat frantic.

"Something's wrong at the lighthouse," he spluttered, "I need someone to come with me, while it's calm."

Robin, grateful for the distraction, dashed to the door and immediately volunteered to accompany Duncan.

"Hold on. You need to rest," Edwin objected. He'd slid out of the alcove after Robin.

Duncan had pulled out a small piece of cloth from his pocket and was wiping the rain from his spectacles. He looked at them both.

"Why? What happened?" he asked, pulling the legs of the eyeglasses behind his ears.

"Nothing, I'm fine. I'm fine, Edwin." Robin shot a look at the red-headed baker that would have quelled the tide. It wasn't that he didn't want Duncan to know. He simply didn't want him to worry. Edwin sighed.

"Fine," he said, "but I'm coming with you."

May Bell was now quite recovered from her earlier ordeal. Her mother had the foresight to bring a change of clothes for the family, and little May was warm and dry in her linen dress, embroidered with woollen flowers and pretty bows. Duncan held the kitten in his hand, clasped gently against his chest. Carefully, he handed the tiny, fragile creature to her.

"Will you look after him for me?" he asked. "I found him all alone among the bramble on the way here."

The little girl was delighted and nodded earnestly. This was not a responsibility she would take lightly.

"He'll probably just sleep, but ask Mr. Reed for a saucer of water for him," Duncan said.

"Water?" she asked. "Don't you mean milk?"

"Oh no, too much cow's milk isn't good for kittens, it can make them ill," Duncan replied quickly. "If he won't drink any water, you can put a couple of drops of milk into it, but no more. Trust me, I used to have lots of cats when I was growing up."

May nodded, and holding the black and white kitten in her arms, she began singing him a lullaby. The kitten gazed up at his new protector and, seemingly finding her care agreeable, closed his bright blue eyes and began to purr.

After his actions earlier, the men of the village seemed more willing to accept Robin's help. Together with Dr. Greenaway, the butcher Mr. Bounsell, and Mr. Blackwall, the fishmonger, they hurried out of the ancient tavern and toward the harbour. The waves had died down considerably, but the journey would still be rough going.

"Where's *Bucca*?" Duncan asked, as he looked toward the little craft's usual mooring place.

"We can't take 'er. We'll 'ave to take one of the luggers or a rowboat," Robin said. "It'll take too long to prepare one of the larger boats."

"What? But we could just..." Duncan began, but Robin was already barking orders at the other men.

A rowboat was resting on the sand, mercifully undamaged but filled with material blown about by the storm. They emptied it out as much as possible and began manoeuvring it into the bay. One by one, they jumped in and positioned themselves at the oars. The rowboat was easily large enough for the six men, and they arranged themselves two to an oar. Robin assumed the captain's role, shouting orders and guiding the inexperienced temporary oarsmen. Once they cleared the harbour, the rain began to spit and they rowed with a new urgency. Before long, Duncan was grumbling about his arms growing tired—not from lack of strength, he hastened to add, but simply from a lack of reach. He was short, barely taller than Mr. Reed, though much broader, and his arms didn't stretch as far as the other men's. Ben Blackwall, who was quite unused to such exertion, was next to useless already, despite his lengthy limbs. Fortunately, Ben had been paired with Edwin, who was more than capable.

As they approached the islet, they spotted their first problem—the tiny wooden pier the keepers used to moor their boat had been swept away, as had the boat itself. The islet was mostly rocks, which presented a significant danger. In calm seas, it would be dangerous to approach, but the winds were blowing again and the waves became rougher with each passing moment. There was a small area to the west of the islet where the rocky shore gave way to a sort of stony beach, but it would be hazardous to attempt a landing there. Robin mulled it over in his mind before deciding they had no other option. Shouting his orders, the men pulled the heavy oars and steered the rowboat around to the side of the jagged isle.

They would have to risk approaching the beach at speed, to avoid being swept into the rocks on either side. There was a chance the craft would be damaged from the stones, but there was nothing else for it. Robin stood at the prow, mooring line in hand, as the village men rowed. The prow struck the beach with terrific force and a hideous scraping sound. As everyone lurched forward from the impact, Robin launched himself through the air at precisely the right moment and landed on the pebbles with a dense thump and mighty grunt. He pulled with all his considerable strength to keep the rowboat swaying from side to side and hitting the huge boulders circling the beach. The other men leapt from the boat and grabbed the mooring line, heaving the tender onto shore. They found a secure rock to tie it to and made their way inland.

Beside the lighthouse had stood a small cottage—the main living quarters for the lighthouse keepers during their tenure on the island. A small, simple, brown building, it had one bedroom and a larger room serving as kitchen, living room, and storage facility. Built shortly after the lighthouse proper, it had withstood many storms over the centuries, but not this one. It had been completely levelled by the hurricane. Rubble lay scattered across the entire islet. Wood, glass, furniture—everything sat in pieces on the ground, a broken trail of breadcrumbs leading to the sea. The men searched quickly for anyone who might have been caught up in the devastation, but finding nothing, they headed for the door of the lighthouse. Painted in red to match the exterior of the lantern room at the summit of the towering edifice, it was shoved open by Duncan, who immediately began to call out to the keepers.

"Keeper Knott? Keeper Hall? Hello, can anyone hear me?"

The ground floor was where the lighthouse keepers stored their wet weather clothes and fishing gear. With no signs of life there, the men from the village made their way up the winding stone staircase. Robin winced from time to time and held his knee. He'd landed heavily on it when he rescued May from the beach, and jumping from the boat hadn't done it any favours. Checking each room as they passed, they found nothing until they reached the second-last floor before the lantern room. Here, a door was barred shut from the inside and they could hear a faint moaning coming from within. They called and banged on the door, but to no avail. Together, Robin and Duncan heaved with all their strength and succeeded in opening the door just enough for the lanky Mr. Blackwall to slip through.

"What can you see?" Mr. Bounsell called.

"Oh dear, oh dear..." Mr. Blackwall said, becoming increasingly panicked.

"What is it? What's happened?" called Mr. Bounsell again.

"Oh dear, oh dear!" came the reply once again, more high-pitched and worried than before.

"Damn it, man, what is it?" Duncan yelled.

"It's Keeper Knott, he's trapped under a heavy bookcase, and he's barely conscious."

"Open the bleddy door!" Duncan roared.

Mr. Blackwall audibly struggled to move the boxes blocking the door and let the other men in. Keeper Hall was sprawled on a stool with his head in one hand and a lantern held loosely in the other. He was swaying as if dizzy, and rambling softly to himself. While Dr. Greenaway examined his head for signs of injury, the other men heaved the fallen bookcase off Keeper Knott. Edwin said that it must have been knocked over by the force of the waves hitting the lighthouse walls. The keeper's leg was broken, so they prepared a splint using some wood from the bookshelves and fashioned a stretcher to carry him downstairs and back to the boat. Keeper Hall had come round a little and was able to walk with some help from Mr. Blackwall, who complained about oil and soot from the lighthouse keeper's hands getting onto his clothes.

"It's bad enough they've already been soiled by those dusty boxes, and what about my poor boots? Soaked through with seawater, they are!"

"That's enough now, Mr. Blackwall," said Robin.

"Books," Keeper Hall said weakly. "Books fell, hit my...hit my head... Wait. Someone has to stay here, to watch the light, to guard the light, to keep it running, to..." He blinked hard, trying to stay awake.

"He's right," Duncan said. "I'll stay." "So will I. You can't do it alone," said Robin.

"I can.You don't always have to..." Duncan began.

"I'll stay too," Edwin interrupted. "If only to keep you two from throwing each other into the sea."

They all helped get the two injured lighthouse keepers downstairs. The winds had picked up again, and they hurried toward to stony beach, picking their way carefully through the remnants of what had been the keepers' cottage. Loading the injured men carefully into the rowboat, they heaved it into the sea and it bobbed along back toward the harbour. Returning to the lighthouse, Robin stood at the door and watched the boat getting farther and farther away, before the waves began to crash again and he was forced to go inside.

"Once they're back on shore, Dr. Greenaway can treat them at the inn," said Edwin.

Robin and Duncan were standing apart, neither one looking at the other.

"For better or worse, we're stranded here for the long haul."

Chapter Twelve

AS THE HURRICANE battered the island once again, the trio made their way up to the lantern room. Each time a powerful wave boomed against the lighthouse, the noise reverberated around the entire structure, causing Edwin to flinch. He felt like each surge brought the tower closer to toppling into the sea. Every slamming assault against the thick walls made him feel small and vulnerable, especially on the lower floors when he knew the waves were reaching high above his head. He felt like he was suffocating. He struggled to catch his breath as he lagged behind the other two men, and had to stop for a moment to gather his resolve. If he could just get above the waves, he'd feel better.

The lantern room was the same size as the other rooms in the lighthouse, but with its conical ceiling and walls made entirely from many small panes of glass, it appeared to be much more spacious. Several cast-iron brackets had been affixed to the metal framework holding the storm panes together. Hanging from some of these—behind the large, rotating beacon—were ceramic pots from which spilled the green and yellow-striped leaves of spider plants. In the centre of the room sat the light mechanism, comprised of a lamp and lens on a copper and brass instrument. Around the circumference of the room was a padded bench, covered with a bright red material the same shade as the lantern room exterior. It was easy to see where the keepers spent most of their time sitting as some areas of this bench behind the lens were heavily worn and cracked.

The bench was unbroken save for where it had to make way for the staircase and the door leading to the metal viewing platform running around the outside of the gallery. This platform was used by the keepers to clean the outside of the windows, and afforded spectacular views of the island. Though not on days like this, of course. Certain sections of the bench were on hinges and could be lifted to reveal storage areas. Edwin reasoned these could easily become cluttered with all manner of unnecessary rubbish, and it must be part and parcel of a lighthouse keeper's duties to keep things as neat and tidy as possible.

It was only once they all reached the lens and watched it catch and reflect the light from the small flame that a thought occurred to Edwin.

"Um, do either of you actually know how to use this contraption?" he asked.

Robin and Duncan exchanged a brief, baffled glance.

"Err, well, Keeper Knott gave me a tour once. I think it's all fairly straightforward. You've got the light and the...glass..." Robin bluffed, rather poorly. He poked around the piping and knowledgably tapped the odd panel and rivet.

"Look," Duncan said, "you put the oil in there. It flows down there—" He traced a pipe coming from a raised reservoir. "—which is lit at the wick there." He pointed to the flame. "The light hits the reflector, which rotates via the mechanism downstairs, and that's all there is to it," Duncan finished, clearly pleased with himself.

"Made a lot of toy lighthouses, have you, Duncan?" Edwin asked, honestly impressed with the knowledge the toymaker had displayed. He wasn't sure if Duncan had gotten it all correct, as there were quite a few pipes and valves left unexplained, but he though it all sounded about right.

"Not working ones..." Duncan mumbled.

"We might 'ave a problem 'ere, boys. Unless I miss my guess, this says the oil's nearly out."

Robin was looking at a gauge on the side of the oil reservoir. Duncan, who had apparently just become an expert lighthouse keeper, double-checked it.

"The keepers must have missed the last refilling time when they were trapped. We'll have to do it."

"Where do they keep the oil?" asked Edwin.

All eyes were on Duncan now.

"Well, they obviously wouldn't keep it up here, too dangerous," blustered Duncan, adjusting the many-lensed spectacles on his little snubbed nose. "It's probably in the room below, the one we passed on the way up."

"The Watch Room, that's called!" Robin loudly declared.

Smiling broadly, he put his hands in his coat pockets and rocked back on his heels, proud to have remembered something from his tour. Edwin thought he looked for all the world like a schoolboy who finally answered a teacher's question correctly. Duncan smiled too, which didn't go unnoticed.

"I'll go have a look," said Edwin.

He found being above the waves, in a room that was essentially a big glass box, created a new problem for him. He was feeling dizzy, as if the whole lighthouse were wobbling from side to side, on the brink of toppling over with every wave that struck. He headed back down the stone steps, happy to no longer be able to see out across the raging waters. Below the lantern room, where the light was housed, was a room where the oil and other items were kept. A selection of battered, well-used handheld lanterns was kept on a shelf, and a logbook sat open on a table. This room had a low ceiling, and though there was still plenty of space, Edwin had the urge to duck slightly as he moved about. The clockwork mechanism—a large shaft with spokes and cogs that rotated the reflector in the room above—ticked noisily in the centre of the room. Other lighthouses were known to use a drum with weighted ropes and a complex series of pulleys and levers running the full length of the structure to achieve rotation, but once again the ingenuity of the Merryapple residents had concocted an alternative.

Edwin glanced at the logbook. Sure enough, there were regular entries made by the keepers indicating when the oil reservoir was topped up. Keeper Knott was a diligent record keeper, it seemed. There were three columns, one for the keeper's name, one marked "Beacon" and another "Mechanism." Each column was filled with either names or times, and going by the regular intervals of the previous entries, it looked like the next entry was overdue. Edwin examined the clockwork shaft in the centre of the room. It had never occurred to him before to wonder how the light actually moved. He wound the instrument a few times until it clicked. Then he picked up the pen, checked the time on his pocketwatch—a gift from his brother some years before—and signed the ledger "Interim Keeper Farriner." The ticking of the mechanism as it turned was far louder down there than in the light room.

On the far wall was a large copper tank with a tap jutting out, and underneath it was something that looked like a watering can. Edwin turned the knob and watched the gooey, pungent whale oil ooze out from the spout and slowly fill the container. As it did so, he thought about the two men upstairs—about that shared smile.

"You waited too long, Edwin." He sighed to himself. "Again."

Chapter Thirteen

AT THE MOTH & Moon, both lighthouse keepers had been quickly put to bed. This unfortunately meant moving the man who Sylvia Farriner had earlier tried to decamp, as he was the least infirm. He resigned himself to not getting a decent night's sleep and joined the rabble in the bar. Dr. Greenaway thoroughly examined the injured men. Keeper Knott's leg was bandaged with a splint, and Keeper Hall's head was attended to as well. His injuries appeared less serious, but Dr. Greenaway knew that could be misleading and he recruited volunteers to keep an eye on the man throughout the night. They were given strict instructions to alert the doctor if they noticed any change in the man's condition, no matter how slight.

During the calm, the inn had welcomed the family Trease, owners of the farm in the northeast of the island. The storm had wrenched the water wheel from the side of their mill, and an errant lightning bolt had started a fire in one of their stables. They had managed to put it out, but not without some difficulty. Once the winds began to die down, Mrs. Trease convinced her obstinate husband to pack up and head to the inn. She was also concerned about the well-being of her sister—the wife of the ailing oysterman, Mr. Hirst—and insisted they call on her on the way to the inn. Relations between the siblings had been strained ever since the younger sister had left the farm. Mrs. Trease had wanted her sister to live with her new husband in one of the converted outbuildings and either work the land or serve in the mill, but Mr. Hirst had fishing in his blood and wouldn't even consider it. And where Tim Hirst went, so went his obedient wife.

Stopping by their modest home on the way to the Moth & Moon, they found Abigail Hirst in an agitated state. She had become increasingly worried about her husband's condition and considered sending one of her daughters to the inn for help. So worried was she that when she opened the door to find her sister standing there, she forgot all about their feud and threw her arms around her neck, sobbing. The family gently put Mr. Hirst on the Trease's cart and then brought him to the tavern where he was laid out in a room on an upper floor. This meant moving someone else from their bed, but when they discovered the reason, they gladly surrendered it.

The eye had passed now and the winds had returned with renewed vigour. Even the great wheel—the Moth & Moon's ancient chandelier—swayed from side to side, flicking pearls of wax as it went. The tavern fell into a frightened hush when they heard a sound quite unlike any other. A frightful splintering, bursting, crashing peal, a thousand times louder, it seemed, than any heard thus far. In the howling darkness, it was impossible to tell what had been lost.

Shortly afterwards, on a southern wall of the inn, a pair of shutters were wrenched free and the window panes they protected were scattered across the room in splinters and shards. Rain mingled with brine and sand streamed in, drenching those nearby. Many hammers and spare nails had been stored behind the bar for just such an occurrence, and before long—but not without difficulty— the villagers used some wooden planks to put up a makeshift barrier across the jagged hole. They did their best, but a slight gap was unavoidable, and the storm whistled as it blew through it.

Morwenna Whitewater's tweed knights had finished their rounds of the inn, gathering up every scrap of news and gossip, and had returned to the round table to share the particulars with her. Morwenna was sitting in her usual spot by the fire when Eva Wolfe-Chase sashayed over to warm her delicate hands; tiptoeing around the children on the mat as she did so.

"Good evening," Lady Wolfe-Chase said with a little bow to the round table. "I saw your altercation with Mrs. Farriner earlier. She's quite the piece of work."

She removed her lace gloves and set them on the crowded mantelpiece before holding her hands out to the roaring flames. Being so close to the front of the building, the splashing of the rain outside sounded even louder, but that couldn't drown out the incessant clacking sound of Mrs. Hanniti Kind's knitting needles.

Morwenna sniffed and fiddled with her cane. "That woman is impossible. Always been the same. Impossible."

"You've known her a long time?"

"Oh yes. Far too long. Since we were girls. She's younger, of course, but she always thought she was more mature than her years. Always stirring up trouble, that one."

"She's not all bad," said Mrs. Greenaway. "She's just highly strung."

The clacking needles paused for a moment as Mrs. Kind stared at her fellow knight.

"That's one way of putting it," sniffed Morwenna.

"I wondered why she wasn't part of your enclave," Eva Wolfe-Chase smiled.

"She used to be," said Mrs. Greenaway, softly.

"For about five minutes. Until it turned out to be a ruse to get at me," Morwenna said. "We thought she'd turned over a new leaf—she was all sweetness and light. Should have known better."

"Good on you for not putting up with her," Eva Wolfe-Chase said. "What did she..."

"Eva! Darling, there you are," said her wife, who took her by the arm and gently led her away from the fire and the round table.

"I hope she wasn't talking your ear off. Or gossiping," Iris Wolfe-Chase said.

"Not at all, we were just discussing life in the village. It must be such a change from life on Blackrabbit," said Morwenna.

"Oh my, yes! It's much more fun!" said Eva Wolfe-Chase said as her wife began leading her away in earnest.

"Lady Wolfe-Chase. Your gloves," Morwenna said, pointing to the mantelpiece with the end of her cane.

"Oh, of course. Thank you, Mrs. Whitewater," she replied.

As the two women left to return to their alcove, Mrs. Greenaway wrinkled her nose. "I think it's a disgrace," she said to no one in particular as she continued her needlework. Since she'd arrived in the Moth & Moon, she'd kept herself busy by working on a needlepoint image of the island. She'd finished the outline of the coast, and was currently filling in the hills.

"What is?" asked Mrs. Kind.

"Those two. I mean, imagine! Getting married. To someone from Blackrabbit Island! There should be a law against it."

On the thick, heavy bar that had once been part of the stern of a mighty sailing vessel, May Bell sat with her legs tucked under her pretty cotton dress. One of the villagers had been kind enough to lift her up and plonk her where she wouldn't be in the way, and wouldn't fall. Behind her was one of the enormous pillars flanking the bar and in front of her was Duncan's rescued animal. She had taken a ribbon from her dress and was dangling it above the kitten's head. He lay on his back, trying to grab it with all four paws. Three of them grabbed it occasionally, but his shortened leg always fell just shy of it. Whenever he caught it, he playfully gnawed on it with tiny, sharp teeth until May yanked it up again and he had to start over.

Mr. Reed was busy drying glasses when he spotted the girl on his countertop. He sauntered over to where she was sitting and leaned against the bar, casually attending to a resolute mark with his cloth.

"Is that a real cat or a ghost cat?" he asked her suddenly.

May sat up straight and gave the grey-bearded tavern keeper a reproachful look.

"There are no ghosts, Mr. Reed. My mummy said so," she said in her most grown-up voice.

Mr. Reed continued cleaning the tankard.

"Oh, right, right. Have you not heard about the ghost cat in the lighthouse? Everybody knows about it. Maybe you're too young to have heard of it." He winked knowingly at the villager who had lifted the girl onto the counter, and who now laughed into his tankard.

May hated when adults did that. They always winked at each other as if she wouldn't notice but she always did. She hated that expression, as well. *Too young.* It got her hackles up. She was almost eleven, more than old enough to hear any kind of story one cared to tell. She gave him her steeliest look.

"I'm not too young. Tell me about it right now!" she demanded, slamming her little fist on the counter and almost tipping over the saucer of water left out for the kitten.

"Well, back along, a lighthouse keeper lived out there with his wife. It was lonely, as it was just the two of them and they had no children, but they had lots of cats."

"Where did the cats come from?" May asked.

"The island, of course. The lighthouse keeper brought one back every time he went ashore in his rowboat for food. He'd walk into the lighthouse and say 'Wife! I'm home and I have another cat!' and she'd be very happy."

This made perfect sense to May. Who wouldn't be happy with an extra cat every once in a while? Her mother wouldn't let her have any cats at home; she said they would make a mess.

"Anyway," Mr. Reed continued, "one day, the lighthouse keeper's wife fell ill, and she had to stay in bed. It was very boring for her as the cats wouldn't stay with her. They preferred to play outside. All except one. A little black and white kitten, a bit like this one." He pointed to the animal.

"This kitten loved to play with a little ball the keeper's wife would throw from her bed out into the staircase. The kitten would chase after it and bring it back."

"Cats don't fetch things, Mr. Reed," May said, folding her arms knowledgeably. "Dogs do."

"Some cats do. Anyway, shush," George Reed replied. "So, every day, for weeks, the kitten would chase this ball and keep the lighthouse keeper's wife happy. But then one day, the wife died."

"Oh, no!" May said, hands over her mouth.

"I know, it's sad, but it was a very long time ago, don't worry. After she was gone, the kitten would go to her room every day and lay on her bed, playing with the ball. Sometimes it would get away from him, and he'd chase after it, but he always brought it back to the same room and onto the same bed. Until the day—a day much like this one, actually, when thunder boomed and lightning struck the lighthouse—the keeper walked into the room and he found the cat had passed away on the very same bed as his wife."

May was riveted now. Even the kitten seemed to be paying attention and watched him with his bright blue eyes. Mr. Reed unstoppered a bottle of water and topped up the saucer.

"And they say that to this day, when the winds begin to howl and the lightning strikes, you can still hear the cat chasing the little ball on the stairs."

May remembered the two keepers had been brought to the inn, and resolved to ask them about the ghost when they felt better. She was absolutely certain ghost *people* weren't real, but her mummy never said anything about ghost *cats*.

Chapter Fourteen

DESPITE THE MAIN light being seen for miles out to sea, it was barely bright enough to read a book by. This was a quirk of the construction and reflection angles that Duncan had tried to explain but Robin couldn't wrap his head around. After Edwin had filled the reservoir, he'd replaced the candles in the small lanterns dotted around the lantern room. He kept his gaze fixed on the floor or on the mechanism.

"We might be 'ere for a while so we should probably get some rest. You two go first. I'll keep watch," said Robin. He could see Edwin was about to object. "I got plenty of rest earlier on," He put one hand on Edwin's broad shoulder. "You've been on the go since before dawn at the bakery. It's well past your bedtime! Go on. There's a bedroom downstairs."

"I dozed for about an hour in the Moth & Moon, but now you mention it, I could do with some proper sleep," Edwin said as he wearily headed down the staircase.

"Close the watch room door on your way past!" Robin called after him. "The tickin' of the mechanism will keep you awake, otherwise. You go too, Duncan."

"No, I'll stay for now. You don't really know what you're doing." Duncan said.

"Neither do you."

"That's...that's..."

"That's what?"

"That's... neither here nor there," Duncan said. "If anything goes wrong, its better you have some help on hand."

Robin relented. He knew neither of them were enamoured with the idea of being stuck in a small room together for hours on end, but needs must.They sat at opposite ends of the bench as the winds roared and the rainwater sloshed down the thick panes of glass. The rotating mechanism tick-tick-ticked incessantly, and they looked anywhere but at each other for what was probably the longest hour of their lives.

"I think this is the most time we've spent in the same room for years." Robin finally broke the silence.

"And whose fault is that?" Duncan snapped, immediately regretting it.

The pain was evident on Robin's face, and the warm candlelight deepened the furrows in his brow.

"No, wait. I...I didn't mean that..." Duncan hung his head and took a deep breath. "Look, we can't just sit here like this all night. I saw a deck of cards in the break room on the way up. I'll go get them."

When he returned with the deck and a box of matches, he asked what game they should play.

"How about strip poker?" Robin joked, trying to ease the tension. "Be like old times."

Duncan just glared at him.

"Piquet it is, then," Robin said, feeling slightly embarrassed.

They used some matchsticks to keep score, and in short time, Duncan's pile was by far the biggest. Robin was many things, but a shrewd card player wasn't one of them. Many times over the years, Duncan had tried to teach him how to better hide what he was feeling, but Robin had never developed the knack, which is why he always used to end up in his smallclothes before Duncan had lost so much as a boot.

"I've been readin' more," Robin said, trying to distract himself from the bad hand he'd been dealt.

"Oh, really?" Duncan replied.

"Yep. Been tryin' to, you know, get better at it. Got a load of books off of Morwenner and found some of Dad's in the attic. It's 'ard goin', mind."

"That's really great, Robin. Keep at it." Duncan smiled. "Is there something wrong?"

"No. What makes you think that?" Robin replied, avoiding eye contact. He grabbed the stack of cards in front of them and began clumsily shuffling them, dropping a couple at every cut. He dealt out a hand, but Duncan refused to play and sat instead with his short arms folded.

"I'm not lifting another card until you explain yourself," he said.

Robin didn't try to argue. "You know my neighbour, Eva Wolfe-Chase? She knows what 'appened to the ship Dad died on. It were a pirate ship, Duncan. A pirate ship." He felt so lost just then.

"Oh, Robin. Does that mean..." Duncan stopped as Robin nodded his head.

"Well, it must do. Why else would 'e be on it? I love my dad, but 'e weren't no paragon o' virtue, and I'm not delusional enough to think 'e were on that ship for 'onourable reasons."

Duncan sat back and tried to understand the ramifications. He understood what Erasmus meant to Robin. Despite what anyone else thought about Captain Shipp, Robin had always looked up to him.

"It's bad enough the village thinks 'e were a murderer, what will they say if they find out 'e were a pirate?" Robin asked.

Duncan could see it wasn't anger on his face—it was disappointment.

"Maybe they have a right to know," Duncan said.

Robin looked shocked. "'Ow can you say that?"

"Well, hiding it from them won't do any good; these things have a way of getting out. How will it look if they find out you knew—that you were protecting him? Do you really need to give them another reason to dislike you?" Duncan said. "I know you're the only one who's allowed to say anything bad about your father, Robin, but the fact is *something* happened to Barnabas Whitewater that night, and now you're saying Erasmus ran off and joined a pirate crew straight afterwards? Can't you see how that looks?"

"Yes, I can see exactly 'ow it looks," Robin said, his voice rising, "which is why I don't want anyone findin' out!"

"The man abandoned you, Robin," Duncan shouted. "It might be time to accept he wasn't much of a—" He stopped himself before he said too much. Then he realised he should have stopped himself far sooner. "Look, I won't tell anyone. And neither will the Wolfe-Chase's, I'm sure."

Robin sat with his elbow resting on the metal framework, his fist covering his mouth. He stared out at the lashing rain. "I appreciate that. It's all a bit much to take in at the moment, what with all this goin' on." He gestured to the storm battering the glass-walled room.

They sat in silence, all thoughts of card-playing cast aside. Soon, Duncan's eyelids started to become heavy, and hearing some movement downstairs, he reasoned that Edwin was awake.

"I think I'll turn in," he said and walked to the staircase.

Without looking up, Robin said, "See you in the morning, Duncan."

Duncan felt a little jab in his heart as he said this. For a split second, it was like old times, and he almost expected Robin to kiss him on the cheek as he went past, like he always used to do. Instead, he walked downstairs, and Robin began tidying away the cards and scooping up the matchsticks.

Edwin was awake and putting on his boots. There were two tiny beds in the cramped, curved room. Duncan removed his jacket and hung it on the spare hook behind the door, then placed his waistcoat on the back of a chair.

"Both still alive, then?" Edwin quipped as he tied his laces.

Duncan eyed the baker. He didn't think it was much of a joke. He wearily sat down on the unused bed. The top few buttons of his shirt were already undone, revealing a tangle of black hair reaching towards his bare throat, and now he rolled up his long, white sleeves, revealing his thickset forearms, which were likewise covered in a morass of dark hair sprouting all the way down to his fingers.

"Just about. Couldn't you sleep?" he asked, kicking off his boots and lying back with his hands behind his head. Even though he saw how unsettled Edwin had been in the lantern room, Duncan could see the eagerness with which he was getting ready to head back upstairs.

"Not really. The storm was keeping me awake, and there was odd tapping noise on the stairs, but I got a couple of hours in," Edwin said as he carefully tucked his shirt into his breeches, fussing over it to make sure it was neat and tidy.

"Are you going to tell him tonight?" Duncan asked nonchalantly.

Edwin stopped in midtuck, and Duncan saw how his question landed like a punch to the gut.

"I don't know what you mean," he said, finishing his adjustments and preparing to leave.

"Yes, you do," Duncan replied, his gaze never shifting from the other man's face. "But I suppose what I really want to know is, why haven't you told him before now?"

They had always been polite to each other, but they were casual acquaintances at best. Duncan intentionally made Edwin feel he was nothing more than a background element to him, nothing but a dot of colour on the canvas that was Duncan's life. But all pretence had suddenly fallen away and the two men found themselves on equal footing for what was probably the first time ever.

Standing in the doorway, Edwin turned to face him.

"Because he's still not over you," he said.

He lifted his coat from the back of the door and went downstairs to the kitchen. Duncan lay there for a moment, wondering if it was more than the noise of the storm he could hear from his bed. Then he turned to face the wall and tried to sleep.

Robin was sitting on the bench in the lantern room, looking out towards the village, quietly humming one of the shanties his father used to sing. With help from the frequent lightning flashes, many of which struck the rod at the top of the lighthouse, he could see towards the beach where he had found May Bell. The old rowboat had been completely submerged now, and the waterline had reached the scrubland behind the sand. It likely wouldn't rise much farther, as the ground inclined sharply there and ran up as a hill, on top of which was the schoolhouse. Higher up lay Duncan's little blue house. Robin shuddered to think what would have happened if no one had found the girl or if he'd waited any longer. With even a few minutes delay, the outcome could have been very different.

A small moth huddled in a corner of the lead framework of the gallery, in what was probably the only sheltered part of the whole assembly. Every now and then, it flexed its wings revealing an iridescent blue the likes of which Robin couldn't remember having seen before. He wanted to open the door and let the poor thing in, but he reasoned that even if it did—and he himself wasn't blown over the edge and down onto the rocks below by the high winds—the moth would probably just fly straight into the open flame of the lighthouse. Damned if you do, damned if you don't, he thought to himself.

Edwin arrived carrying two mugs of tea. Robin thanked him and beckoned him to sit close by him on the bench, which he did. Certainly closer than Duncan had sat.

"You and Duncan seem to be getting on," Edwin said after a little while.

Robin gave a small laugh. "To a point."

They sat for some time, talking about the storm and the damage it might bring. Every once in a while, a huge wave pounded the sea-facing part of the lighthouse and cover even the lantern room gallery in spray. The whole lighthouse boomed with the force of these waves. Robin noticed Edwin had stopped flinching when they struck, but also that he still kept his eyes off the storm panes. Edwin saw him staring.

"What?" he asked.

Robin chuckled slightly, then threw one arm around Edwin's shoulders, grabbed him with both hands, and shook him a little.

"Don't worry, Mr. Farriner, I won't let you fall!" He laughed.

Edwin laughed a little too, but blushed more.

"Is it very obvious?" he said, flicking drops of tea off his legs. Robin's shaking had dislodged several spashes of liquid from Edwin's cup.

"I've seen that look before, mostly in new sailors who're daunted at the prospect of climbin' a ship's riggin'. It's nothin' to be ashamed of," Robin said.

"Were you ever nervous doing that?" Edwin asked.

"Oh, no. Well, at first, I suppose I was, a bit, but you get used to it. I didn't 'ave to do it much. Weren't long enough on those big ships."

"I always wondered about that. You love being on the water so much; I'm surprised you didn't sign on for a life at sea."

"I tried it for a while. Almost as soon as I left I wanted to return 'ome. I were lucky. Thanks to Dad, I didn't 'ave to stay away. I suppose I didn't care much for the big, wide world. My world is 'ere." Robin smiled.

Edwin nudged his shoulder. "You soppy tuss." He laughed.

After a while, Edwin fell silent and Robin watched him intently. Edwin's eyes had become deeper, sadder somehow, and he was rubbing his freckled forearm absent-mindedly.

"Somethin' on your mind?" Robin asked.

"I'm...worried about my bakery. If it's damaged in this storm, it's my livelihood on the line; I won't be able to look after Mum and Dad. I keep thinking about how far behind I'll be if this storm keeps up. Eva suggested I take on an apprentice," Edwin gathered his coat closer around himself.

"It's not a bad idea. You know I worry about you doin' all that work yourself."

Edwin looked at his friend, who had turned to face him, watching him in the wan candlelight.

"I know you feel like you're still in your brother's shadow. You're still tryin' to live up to 'im. To 'onour 'im. But you're not goin' to do that by workin' yourself into an early grave. Please now, Edwin, an apprentice is a good idea—promise me you'll at least consider it?"

Robin's voice had become low and serious. The gruffness was gone, and he had unknowingly leaned in closer. Edwin watched his pale lips curve and throb.

"I promise," he said. "I know I've been pushing myself. I just feel..."

"Like you should be able to do it all?"

"I suppose."

"Well, you 'ave done it all. You've been doin' it all for, what, eight years now? Let someone 'elp ease the pressure. If you burn yourself out, who'll be left to run the bakery then?"

Edwin nodded and managed a thin smile. "Speaking of work, you must be worried about *Bucca's Call*?"

Robin's head sank a little, and he avoided Edwin's gaze.

"What is it? What's—?" Edwin began, and then it dawned on him. "Oh, Robin. When you collapsed earlier, that shield you had tied around your arm—it was a piece of *Bucca's Call*, wasn't it? I'm so sorry. I didn't realise..." He placed his hand on his friend's knee.

Robin felt Edwin was the only one who truly understood what the little boat had meant to him. It wasn't just a source of income; it was a link to his past, a refuge, and silly as it sounded, a companion.

"Nothin' to be done about it now." Robin shrugged, obviously upset.

He sat back against the glass again, smiled away his pain, and tried to put on a brave face. He pushed those feelings down, deep down inside of himself, and felt them tighten the knot. When he stood up and made his way to the staircase, he stopped and nervously tapped the banister.

He thought about the decrepit old rowboat on the beach, sunk beneath the punishing waves, and without making eye contact with his friend, he simply said, "I am, you know."

"You are what?" Edwin asked, confused.

"Over 'im," Robin replied with a quick smile before he walked down the stone steps.

He walked past the bedroom and saw Duncan was awake—and listening.

Chapter Fifteen

IT WAS LATE now, and most of the people sheltering at the inn had fallen asleep. The music had stopped, and what little conversations that were left had taken the form of hushed whispers in barely lit corners. The wind had returned with a vengeance, and rain once again battered the ancient tavern.

Mr. Reed sat on a leather chair by a small, oval table. This room, tucked away down a maze of corridors and antechambers, was left untouched by the villagers as it was much too small to sleep in. The room was roughly circular in shape and each wall was fitted, floor to ceiling, with bookshelves stuffed with all manner of tomes from across the world. Many sailors passed through the Moth & Moon over the centuries and had left behind works by authors from every corner of the globe. They ended up here, neatly sorted in cherrywood cabinets. A tall ladder was set against one of them. This was attached to some brass runners circumnavigating the room, allowing it to freely slide around the shelves to where it was needed, then lock into place. Most visitors needed it to gain access to only the highest shelves, but the pint sized Mr. Reed needed it to reach rather more.

A carefully guarded flame flickered in an iron fireplace. This room would be the worse place for a spark to escape, but it would be much too cold to sit in without a fire.

The floorboards were covered with a single large, round rug, elaborately patterned in red and greens, and fringed with tassels. It was a gift from a grateful sailor—and former lover—from a faraway land many moons ago. It was once so vibrant but now worn and faded, especially in front of the two chairs. Between the two high-backed chairs sat a small table, on which were a lantern, a decanter of brandy, two tumblers, and a small box with a glass lid. The box held three pinned moths. Each one was brown with black and grey markings, and each one was subtly different from the last. Mr. Reed was idly flicking through the pages of a book, looking at meticulously drawn illustrations of insects and trying to match them to his latest finds when he became aware of movement in the corridor behind him.

"Come in, Lady Wolfe-Chase," he said.

She glided into the tiny room at the centre of the warren and settled into the opposite chair.

"If you're sure I'm not disturbing you." She sparkled.

"Not at all. I couldn't sleep; I just needed a bit of a break." Mr. Reed poured a small amount of brandy from the crystal decanter into each glass. Eva Wolfe-Chase lifted hers and flamboyantly clinked it against Mr. Reed's.

"Cheers," she said, and they both took a sip.

"Have you come to make another offer on the inn?" Mr. Reed said bluntly.

She smiled. There weren't many people on this island who shared her predilection for getting to the point.

"No, I haven't. Although from what I've seen, tonight would be the best time to make one. You seem particularly troubled this evening."

Mr. Reed swirled the liquid around in his glass as she lifted the display box from the table.

"I gather it's been in your family for a long time."

"Oh yes, quite a few generations. Did you know it predates the village?"

"What? Really? I thought that was just a bit of colourful local lore?"

"No, not at all. Four hundred years ago, or thereabouts, a ship passing by the then-uninhabited Merryapple found itself blown into the cove by a storm and smashed upon the rocks. People had been visiting the island for centuries, of course, but no one had ever settled here. It was a little too remote, I suppose. Too small. Anyway, the surviving sailors stripped the wreckage and used its parts to build what would one day come to be known as the Moth & Moon. It was much smaller back then, of course. The sailors had built nothing more than a large shack, thinking they would be rescued before too long. It's been added to a great many times since, but even today, you can see elements of that ship in the walls and ceiling of the inn. The massive posts in the central bar area—and the bar itself—all used to be part of the framework of the ship. The chandelier hanging above the main seating area in front of the bar was originally the ship's wheel."

Mr. Reed had told this story many times before, and rattled off these facts with practised ease.

"While the sailors waited to be rescued, they explored the island and found it pleasant enough, with extensive woodland and space for farmland, which would be sheltered from the harsh sea winds by hills. The embryonic Moth & Moon came to be the hub of a burgeoning settlement. It had been used as a drinking establishment from the get-go, given that the sailors had managed to salvage several barrels of rum and whiskey and had little else to while away the time awaiting rescue. When some ships did eventually come, most of the sailors decided to remain, sending for their families to join them, as well as for other materials necessary to start a new village. As for what to do with the shack, it seemed only natural to continue to use it as an inn once they decided to stay.

"They found the island had two things in abundance—apple trees and many varieties of beautifully patterned moths. The apples made for a particularly nice cider, as I'm sure you've discovered. No one knows who exactly it was that named the inn, though several local families have stories claiming it was their ancestor—Hanniti Kind will offer her clan's version to anyone who'll listen after she's had a few—but the name has never changed in all the years since. Ownership of the tavern, however, changed several times throughout the generations, finally ending up in the hands of my family. And now my hands. And as for the future; who knows? Maybe it will all end with me."

Mr. Reed took a mouthful of liquid from his glass as Eva watched him intently. That last part wasn't in his usual spiel, it just spilled out of him. Too many brandies, perhaps.

"These moths you catch," she asked, examining the little display case. "Why do you do it?"

Mr. Reed thought about it for a moment.

"Because they're beautiful," he said at last. "Because I want to...know them, I suppose. Recognise them. They're different now, did you know that? When I was a boy, there were these lovely big blue moths on the north of the island. They're all gone now. Nobody's seen them in years. So, I want to catch the species that are around now and preserve them for...posterity, I suppose you'd call it. At least that way, I'll be of some use to future generations. I won't have wasted my time. I'll have something to show for my life."

Mr. Reed swirled his glass again before swallowing the brandy. Eva Wolfe-Chase sat the box and her glass back down on the little table.

"Come with me," she said, rising to her feet.

She took Mr. Reed by the hand and led him through the bewildering tangle of lantern-lit corridors. Turning left and right and left again, up a handful of steps, and down some others. Over carpets, over mats, over naked floorboards. Past the ornately decorated rooms with gorgeously patterned wallpaper and carved furniture, past the sparsely decorated rooms with bare wooden walls and simple stools. Past the antechambers filled with exhausted villagers sleeping head-to-toe and shoulder-to-shoulder, and past the alcoves filled with even more. She trailed him out into the main bar, tiptoeing through the assembled, snoring masses. Lightning flashed and thunder roared. She stood behind the diminutive innkeeper, resting her delicate hands on his shoulders, and then she leaned down and spoke to him.

"Look around you, Mr. Reed," she whispered. "The whole village is here. Without you, without this place, they'd be in danger. In their storm-battered homes, lying alone or afraid or injured or worse. But instead they're here, in the shelter of this place, in the safety you provide for them. You're the caretaker for the whole community, the keeper of its stories—one of many, in a long line of custodians. A link in a vitally important chain. You've given your life in service of this island, of its people. That is not a waste of time. That is something to be proud of. There are many people who would give everything they have for such clarity of purpose. You are the keeper of the Moth & Moon. You matter, Mr. Reed."

Chapter Sixteen

IT WAS BEFORE dawn, and Robin had finally admitted defeat and gone to bed, leaving Duncan and Edwin to keep watch in the lantern room. They had hardly spoken a word to each other in hours. Duncan sat whittling a piece of wood he'd picked up from the supplies on the ground floor. He was using a knife he always kept in one of his seemingly bottomless coat pockets. As Edwin watched the splinters fall into a bucket by the toymaker's feet, a feline shape slowly emerged.

"A cat?" he asked at last.

"Yes. I used to carve them when I was growing up on the farm," Duncan replied without breaking his rhythm and, he felt to his credit, without rolling his eyes.

"Oh, I didn't know you were raised on a farm."

Duncan saw this for what it was, of course—a transparent attempt to get him to open up, to make a connection between them. To break the tension. Under other circumstances, he probably wouldn't have cooperated, but there was something about Edwin he liked, much as he tried to deny it. He had an openness to him. It was a trait he'd noticed was shared by many on this island, quite unlike their neighbours to the north. If he was being honest, Duncan would say he was feeling a little guilty for how he'd ambushed Edwin earlier that night. He had a tendency to act first and think later.

"I wasn't exactly a natural farmer, not like my brothers were," Duncan said, continuing his carving. "I was the youngest of five. Well, I mean, I still am. My brothers all took to farming from the moment they could walk. All I wanted to do was make things. I carved constantly, every free moment I had. I used any scrap of wood I could find. Our farm was beside a large forest so there was always a good supply. Anything that didn't go for firewood, I squirrelled away to practice on."

Edwin leaned in from the other side of the bench on which they were sitting.

"You're very talented," he said.

"My father didn't think so. He wasn't pleased that I was devoting so much time and energy to it. He wanted me to be like him, to work the land, to use my hands like a man. When I told him I was still working with my hands, he...well, he didn't take it well. My brothers all took his side, as usual. When I wasn't getting berated by him, I was getting mercilessly teased by them."

"What did your mother have to say about it?" Edwin asked.

"My mother died giving birth to me, and I don't think my father ever really forgave me. We tried to reach a compromise. He said if I liked carving so much maybe I should apprentice with a carpenter—put my skills to some use." Duncan blew some wood dust from what was fast becoming a cat's ear.

"We had a carpenter who worked on the farm, so my father arranged for me to apprentice under him. Which I did, for a few years, but I got bored. I liked making furniture, that wasn't so bad, but that sort of work was rare. Mostly, it was just repairing carts or preparing joists. I tried to inject some creativity into the work, but it was usually rejected by the master carpenter and word invariably got back to my father who would give me an earful, or worse. He kept telling me people didn't want fancy things, I should just be happy to do things the way they've always been done. Well, I just couldn't do that. I kept carving in my free time and built up a small collection of animals. I fashioned models of our cats, our sheep, horses...anything, really."

Duncan had stopped sculpting now. He sat staring at his reflection in the glass walls of the lighthouse gallery. He saw himself as he was back then—young but older than his years, short and brawny, dark hair cut tight as his father had always insisted. And unhappy. So unhappy.

"One day, I came back from collecting wood in the forest and found my father burning all of my carvings in a fire in the yard. He said he was sick of seeing them. That they were a 'frivolous distraction.' My brothers stood and watched silently; then they threw the last of them on the blaze. Right there and then, I packed my clothes and walked away from the farm, and I haven't been back since. The only thing he didn't burn was a little robin, because I always carried it with me, in my pocket. It was my favourite. So when I came here to Merryapple, and I met a man named Robin, well, I couldn't help but take it as a good sign."

Edwin smiled at this, and there it was again. That charming sort of innocence, that unguarded display. Duncan was beginning to see, aside from his obvious physical charms, why Robin liked him so much.

"I would have thought the same thing," Edwin said. "That's when you moved to Blackrabbit?"

"Yes. The farm was on the mainland, and I just wanted to get away, so I moved to Blackrabbit Island. I found a furniture maker there who was willing to take me on. I spent my days making cabinets and tables and chairs, carving intricate legs, elaborate cornicing, and so on. Exactly the kind of thing my father would have dismissed as pointless extravagances. When I found time, I made toys. Turned out I was good at it and I enjoyed it. Eventually, I started my own business. I made a decent living, bought a house, and was happy for a while. Unfortunately, I got into a bad relationship that ended poorly and left me in debt. I was too in love to see how I was being used. He was the son of a prominent businessman with political aspirations, which complicated things greatly."

"Sorry, who had political aspirations, him or his father?"

"Both, as it turned out. I had to sell my home and my business. I took what I had left and moved again."

"So, then you came here?"

"Yes. The day I moved here was the day I met Robin. I was so blown over by him. Well, technically, I was knocked over by him—you've heard the story—you know what I mean. My last relationship had been a nightmare by the end. I never knew what was happening, what to say, what to do. Every little thing was twisted and turned and thrown back in my face. It ended over a year earlier. It took that long to untangle myself from it."

"Sounds horrible," Edwin said.

"To say the least. So, to go from that to meeting Robin, someone who was so open and so honest and so caring it was a revelation. It's no wonder I fell for him so quickly."

He reached into the pocket of his midnight-blue overcoat, which rested on the bench next to him, and pulled out another small carving tool. This one was curved slightly at the end to create a smoother finish in the woodwork. As he did so, a piece of paper fell out of the pocket and landed on the floor beside Edwin's feet, who bent down and picked it up. Duncan wondered if he'd recognise the distinctive scrawl on the note as being Robin's handwriting, and what he might say if he did. Edwin's face gave nothing away and he simply handed the paper back. Duncan made a mental note never to play poker with him and tucked the note away, deep inside the pocket. He was mad at Edwin for giving nothing away in his expression, and madder at himself for having dropped it in the first place. He adjusted the armatures on his gold-rimmed glasses, flicking one of the tiny lenses into position. This magnified the finer details of his carving, enabling him to achieve a better finish.

"Those glasses of yours, I've never seen anything quite like them," Edwin said.

"No, you wouldn't have. They're my own design—an idea that came to me one night as I was trying to paint tiny patterns onto a piece of dollhouse furniture. I drew up some plans and took them to Mr. Wolfe, the blacksmith. He huffed and puffed and said it wasn't possible, that the joints needed to operate the armatures would be too small, too fine, to ever properly work, and it wasn't worth wasting time on. Luckily, his nephew, Albert, had overheard us talking and wasn't quite so dismissive. While Mr. Wolfe was concerned with things like wheels, axels, and horseshoes, Albert sees himself as a jeweller—interested in creating works of beauty, instead of practicality.

"He poured over my plans and for a few weeks, we worked closely together to create the final pair of glasses. Each lens is of a different strength, different magnification, and can be slotted into place and adjusted and twisted and combined in dozens of variations to achieve different results. I had originally envisioned using them only when I was working, but given that I seem to spend most of my time working on some piece or other, I eventually took to wearing them all day, every day.

"Albert and I have a lot in common, and we soon became friends. Just the other day, we were in the Moth & Moon discussing the possibility of him opening his own jewellery business on Hill Road. I really believe there's a demand for work of the kind of quality he's capable of, and I think he could easily sell his work on Blackrabbit Island, too. He taught me how to make the wind-up mechanisms for my toys.

"I don't think I know him. I'm sure I've seen him around, though," Edwin said.

"Oh, you would have done, he's a bit taller than me, slimmer, walks with a cane? Some accident involving a horse when he young."

"Is he the one married to Mrs. Kind's niece?" Edwin asked.

"No, no, he was engaged to a young woman until she broke off their arrangement and left the island. Albert was devastated, threw himself into his work. Mr. Wolfe said I brought his nephew out of his shell, breathed some life back into him. I don't know about all that. I just felt I was returning the favour for a friend. After Robin and I ended our relationship, it was the friendship and support of Albert, and Hamilton Bounsell for that matter, which had helped me through."

"You weren't tempted to move again? After it ended?" Edwin asked, delicately.

"No. Not really," Duncan said. "It was awkward, as first, when we parted ways. It's a small village so I'd see him almost every day. But it was worth it. I love living here."

Duncan turned the cat model over in his small, fuzzy hands, inspecting it for any imperfections, any areas that could be improved. He found none.

"I heard you talking last night. Some of it, anyway," Duncan said, causing Edwin to blanch. "It's fine, don't worry. It wasn't easy to hear what Robin said, but I think I needed to hear it. I didn't leave the island because I think, for all the pain after we separated, I couldn't bring myself to be completely apart from him."

He sat the wooden cat on the bench, facing out towards the storm-battered village.

"I just wish that if it had to end, that it could have ended differently. Ended better."

Chapter Seventeen

LATER THAT MORNING, while they waited for Edwin to return with the next refill of oil, Robin and Duncan stood in silence. The flame from the giant lamp flickered and danced as the wind howled and the rain battered the thick, aged glass of the lantern room. It may have been morning, but the sky was filled with heavy, grey clouds, and the light was still dim.

"You know," Duncan began, looking around the glass-walled room, wrought from steel and iron, cast with bronze mechanisms, and centred around a pillar of flame and mirrors, "in another time, this would almost be romantic."

Robin recognised this as Duncan's attempt to raise a smile and assuage his guilt for any damage his careless words had caused the night before.

"Yes," said Robin, avoiding his gaze. "Almost."

"What happened between you two?" came a voice from behind them. Edwin had seen this exchange from the top of the staircase. He carried the copper container, now brimming with greasy whale oil for the lamp. "You were so good together, but then you couldn't bear to be around each other. I know it's none of my business, but no one knows what happened."

Robin and Duncan looked at each other. Robin wanted to run away; every fibre of his being was screaming. He'd spent so long both wanting to have and trying to avoid this very conversation. In the past, he'd waited for Duncan to take the first step, but he never did, and so it gnawed away at him. The knot tightened. In his bed in the Moth & Moon, he'd resolved to speak to Duncan, to try to iron out what happened between them—but not now, not now, it was much too soon—he didn't have time to think, time to find the right words, but it was happening right now, right here, in front of Edwin.

They had parted ways over two and a half years before, but they had never hashed out their differences. Never talked about what went wrong. There would be no better time to resolve it than now, but what if he pushed it too far? What if it just deepened the rift between them?

"We drifted apart," said Duncan, suddenly, his gaze fixed on the floor. "His work took him away early each morning; mine kept me up all night. We hardly saw each other, and even when we did, we'd hardly talk, except to argue. Whatever connection we had, whatever force brought us together, it wasn't strong enough to keep us together. It wasn't strong enough to overcome real life, I suppose." He lifted his head and addressed Robin directly now. "You wouldn't accept anything was wrong, that anything had changed. You found it so hard to let go. You made me say it."

The pain was back in Robin's expression. Suddenly, he felt all of his years rushing through his bones. All the wear and tear of his work pulsing in his joints, the weight of his life on his back. He stepped back, wobbling slightly as he slumped down onto the bench. His mouth hung open as he struggled to speak. Why did Edwin have to ask that now? Couldn't it have waited? He wasn't ready. Wasn't prepared. More time, he needed more time; couldn't he have waited just a little longer? But he had to speak now. Right now.

"I didn't mean to, Duncan. I swear, I didn't know that's what I was doin'."

Duncan sighed. "I know, Robin, but you did it regardless."

Tears filled Duncan's eyes, but he blinked them away.

"It made me the villain. It created an...air...around us. An aura. People in the village were reacting to it without knowing why. For weeks after, people treated me differently, because I was still the newcomer. You had the history, you had the connection, and I was just someone who wandered in, uninvited. Until they realised I wasn't going anywhere—that I was staying in the village. And even now, whenever we're together, we go right back to that day. Right back to me as the enemy. And damn it, Robin, it's not fair. I didn't deserve that. I don't deserve that."

Duncan turned away from Robin and stood facing the island. "Why did you ever even fall for me in the first place?" he asked in a hushed tone.

"When you first came 'ere, you were so different," Robin said after a moment's thought. "So lost. Your eyes were so sad, but when we were together, you came alive. You were so 'andsome when you smiled. And you needed me. For the first time in my life, someone actually needed me."

"So, it was pity? You felt sorry for me?"

"O' course not, don't be so... Why do you always 'ave to do that? You asked me, and I'm tryin' to explain. Bein' around you made me feel good. Made me feel useful. Wanted. You were so different from everyone else in the village. You didn't know anythin' about my past, didn't judge me by it the way everyone else does—is it really any surprise I fell in love with you? I never wanted to 'urt you, Duncan."

"I know, Robin, I know. Despite what some people in this village think, you don't have a malicious bone in your body. You may not be the sharpest knife in the drawer, but you're the kindest, most gentle man I've ever met. The thing is, though, no matter how hard you try, no one gets to go through life without hurting someone else."

In the silent expanse that followed, Robin realised how much Duncan had needed to say these things. And, in his heart of hearts, he realised how much he had needed to hear them.

Outside, the wind had begun to die down. The waves that had reached almost to the lantern room now hit only half as high. The lightning strikes on the rod at the top of the lighthouse were less frequent. All of this went unnoticed by the three men in the lantern room. "You're right. You don't deserve it," Robin said at last. "I'm sorry, Duncan. I'm sorry for lettin' that 'appen. I didn't know what to do. I didn't want to accept that things were goin' wrong between us. When I met you, it felt like I'd been lookin' for you my whole life, only I didn't realise it. I waited so long to find you, I couldn't let you go. Rose left me. Dad left me. I didn't want to you leave me too. But you did. Everyone does."

Robin was trembling now, unsure of what to say until it came tumbling out of his mouth. He thought about the years they had spent together. Five brief, wonderful years. He thought about the winter they met, when he had slipped on an icy patch and slid down the steep road right into Duncan, knocking him off his feet on his very first day in the village. The following yuletide, on their first anniversary, when Duncan had given him a model of *Bucca's Call* that he spent weeks crafting in his workshop. He thought of their last winter together when Duncan had finally had enough, had enough of never seeing him, never talking. All of it came flooding back with crystal clarity. No more fooling himself that it was something that just happened, something unavoidable, no more falsehoods. He saw everything as it truly was.

"I did love you, Robin. With all my heart and soul, I loved you, and I watched you drift away from me."

Duncan sat on the bench, close to Robin.

"I loved you too," Robin said in a quivering, muted tone. "I 'ope I said that enough, I 'ope you knew what you meant to me, what it meant to come 'ome to you every day. What it meant to 'ave you near."

"This is the first time you've apologised," Duncan said, "but you never had to. It's not about blame. I know I'm not the easiest person to talk to at times, but this is all we really needed, Robin. To talk. All you ever had to do was meet me halfway."

"I waited too long. I always do. I wait and I wait, and I expect things to work themselves out. I waited for you to fix us, and when you didn't, when you couldn't...I didn't know what to do. I..."

"...gave me no choice."

Robin took a deep breath. "No, I didn't, did I? No choice at all."

As they sat in the lamp room of the battered lighthouse, the waves that had crashed so violently against it seemed to temper their anger, the winds that howled mercilessly became mere whispers, and the rain that pounded the village eased to drizzle.

Edwin stood back and watched as Robin carefully unlocked the door leading out to the platform running around the outside of the gallery. While some grey clouds remained, the colour that had been stolen from the world at the onset of the storm was returning. The murky olive of the fields had given way to vibrant green, and the sallow ivory of the houses was yielding to brilliant white. Robin tested the walkway with a few pokes of his boot to be sure it hadn't come loose in the storm before gingerly stepped out onto the metal framework, followed by Duncan. Edwin nervously approached the doorway. Robin held out his hand and smiled reassuringly.

"Come on. It'll be fine. I won't let you fall."

Edwin grasped his warm hand tightly, took a deep breath, and stepped outside. The air was cold and tasted saltier than usual. He kept his gaze straight ahead—facing the village—and held fast to the railings. He was surprised when he felt Duncan's hand low on his back, steadying him, assuring him it was safe.

From their vantage point, they had an unobstructed view of the devastation wrought by the hurricane.

Chapter Eighteen

IT WAS APPROACHING noon as Robin, Duncan, and Edwin left the lighthouse, stubbled and bleary-eyed. They'd eaten a paltry breakfast, which Edwin had prepared for them in the cramped kitchen. None of them had felt particularly hungry, not even Robin, but Edwin had insisted they eat something to keep their strengths up. It had been a long night, and he said the day ahead would be longer still.

Some fishermen came to collect them and drop off a couple of villagers to take over their duties. The people of Blashy Cove would need to work out a schedule to cover the lightkeeping duties while the keepers recuperated, but there would be time for that later. For now, there were plenty of volunteers. The fishermen arrived in a badly damaged lugger—the masts had been cracked and the sails torn off. They managed to row it by hand, but it was slow going. The three men, weary though they were, all pitched in with the rowing on the way back.

They stopped at the pier, in the same spot where Robin usually moored *Bucca's Call*, and climbed up the wet stone steps where they surveyed the damage caused the storm. Many houses had damaged roofs and chimney pots. Trees had been uprooted, windows had been smashed, branches and glass were scattered everywhere. Some carts, which hadn't been properly secured, were smashed to smithereens. Wood was strewn everywhere, planks and timber frame piled like matchsticks. Clothes and bedding snatched from damaged homes were snagged on posts, then torn and shredded, left flapping in the breeze like ragged flags. A large lugger known as a jumbo had been lifted by the surging tide and deposited yards up the beach. It sat there, listing to one side like a beached whale, mast snapped in half. Dogs howled in the ruins of homes, digging for lost artefacts. The Wishing Tree—valiant sentinel of the Merryapple headland—had stood for centuries, but even it was shaken, its roots partially tugged from the ground, and sat now like a loose tooth. Roads had been cracked open, marbled by the shifting soil beneath. This upheaval was most noticeable around the forge, which sat slumped on one side where the walls had partially subsided. Huge cracks ran across every surface, deep spiderwebs shattering the plasterwork.

The worst of the damage was caused at the bend in Hill Road, past Edwin's bakery. Several premises had been completely obliterated, but the most keenly felt for the village was the loss of the sea-green establishment that had stood at the bend in the road. The Painted Mermaid Museum & Tea Room was no more. It was just possible to see amid the rubble and debris the footprints of where these structures had once stood. The buildings themselves—reduced to splintered, component parts—had been deposited up the hills and down the far side, all the way to the orchard and out across the beaches and waters to the west of the island. The shops they had been attached to stood exposed to the elements, from ground to roof, like giant dollhouses. Open wounds in the flesh of the village.

Though the rain had stopped, every surface was still drenched. Enormous puddles had gathered in places, and small, muddy rivers ran from the top of the hills, down every road, path, and laneway and into the cove. As they walked toward the village in silence, Robin looked back at the pier. It was largely undamaged. Most of the bigger boats moored in the bay were still afloat, though every mast had been broken in some way. Smaller vessels had been washed up onto the beach, and while each one had sustained some manner of damage, none appeared to be completely unsalvageable.

They walked to the seafront where Duncan and Edwin stood as Robin searched through the rubble for signs of his little boat. Under a pile of snapped wood and crab pots, he spotted the flaking crimson prow of *Bucca's Call*. She was on her side, partly buried in the sand. The port side was visible down to about the halfway point. The rear section of the boat was entirely missing, as were both of her masts. He walked the length of the remaining hull, rubbing his hand along it as he did. When he reached the jagged, splintered end, he kept walking, and after a couple of steps, he bent down to dig something out of the wet sand. A plank of wood onto which was bolted a nameplate with several letters missing. He returned to the wreck and laid the slab on top.

Duncan was beside him and placed a hand on his shoulder. "Robin. I'm so sorry..."

Robin looked at him, then to the damaged village beyond. People were leaving the Moth & Moon and discovering what they had lost.

"Doesn't matter now. There's people who've lost more than an old boat," he said with a forced smile. And with that, he strode up the beach towards the inn.

Inside the Moth & Moon, Robin went to see Morwenna Whitewater. He'd seen the damage to her cottage already and told her she was staying with him until her roof was repaired. Edwin went to check on his parents, and found his mother haranguing his father for not finding them more comfortable places to sleep. Nathanial wasn't listening. A night spent propped up against an uneven wall had given him a crick in his neck, which he was trying to rub and roll away.

Duncan found May and her mother sitting near the big fireplace. Looking around for the little kitten, May giggled and pointed to the large mantelpiece where he had made himself at home amongst the knick-knacks decorating it. He purred contentedly as Duncan stood at the inglenook, reached up on tiptoe, and stroked him under the chin.

"Mr. Hunger," Louisa said, "May has something she wants to ask you."

May shyly stepped forward. "You were in the lighthouse all night? Did you see any ghost cats?"

"Ghost cats?" Duncan laughed. "Well now, let me think. I don't remember seeing any. Although...huh." He thought for a moment.

May blinked and held her hands clasped tightly in front of herself.

"Come to think of it, Mr. Farriner did hear something strange. A sort of tapping, bouncing noise on the staircase."

May gasped at this and immediately ran off to find Mr. Reed and tell him the good news. Duncan and Louisa laughed.

"I'm ever so grateful she's over her ordeal," her mother said.

Duncan looked perplexed for a moment, trying to think if there's something he should know about May, something he should remember. Coming up with nothing, he asked what she meant.

"Didn't you hear? She was caught out in the storm, on the beach. Mr. Shipp rescued her. Did he not tell you?"

Duncan was taken aback by this. "No, not a word."

Louisa smiled and related the whole story to him as they both sat by the glowing embers of the fire. Around them, villagers were packing up their belongings, folding blankets, and more than one of them was nursing a sore head. Duncan presumed they'd made full use of the facilities throughout the night. He lifted the kitten and sat with it resting in his arms, listening to Louisa. He knew now why Edwin had been so concerned that Robin rest and not leave the inn to go to the lighthouse, and why he was keeping such a close eye on him. At least, that was part of the reason. Duncan started to feel worse about how he had spoken to Edwin, and he hit upon an idea how to make it up to him.

"May's grown very fond of that cat," Louisa said.

"I can see why. He's a little darling. Poor thing is all alone now." Duncan smiled down at the tiny furry face resting on his hand.

May was back by her mother's side. As she reached over to stroke the kitten, Duncan lifted him over to her.

"I think he belongs to you," he said.

May looked confused as she stared first at the kitten, then at her mother, then back at Duncan.

"But Mummy doesn't like cats," she said.

"Oh, I think I can make an exception for this one!" Louisa laughed

May chewed the inside of her cheek. Duncan thought it made her little face look funny, like an old man chomping on the end of a pipe.

"Actually, Mr. Hunger, I think Bramble wants to go home with you," she said at last. "I don't think our dog would like him, anyway." Duncan beamed and held the kitten up, looking at him eye to eye.

"Bramble?" he asked.

"It's his name. He told me so," May said quite matter-of-factly.

"Oh, well, very good," he laughed, leaning back in his chair. "Hello, Bramble."

The kitten meowed in reply.

"Thank you very much, May. Actually, I have something for you. A swap, you might say."

He reached into one of the pockets of his luxurious overcoat and drew out the wooden cat he'd spent the night carving. He handed it to the girl who clutched it to her chest.

"I love her!" she exclaimed and turned to show her mother.

Louisa leaned in and hugged her daughter.

"That was very kind of you, giving Mr. Hunger the kitten like that," she said.

May twirled a lock of hair in her fingers. "Frankly, I think he needs the company," she said, leaving Duncan and Louisa laughing uproariously at her bluntness while she ran off to play with her friends.

At the cavernous fireplace, Robin was talking to Morwenna. She was packing her things and preparing to return home.

"We'll call at my 'ouse first, get you settled, and then—" Robin began.

"No, we won't do anything of the kind. I want to see first-hand what's happened to my cottage."

Robin tilted his head. "I really don't think that's a good idea, Morwenner. It will be very upsettin'."

She drew herself up to her full height, all five feet nothing of it, and stomped her walking cane on Robin's left boot, causing him to hop back.

"Robin Jonas Shipp, I have survived being shipwrecked, widowed, and now one hurricane. I will survive seeing some damage to a house."

Robin wondered if perhaps she was fretting about the harm that might have come to her late husband's paintings and wanted to check on them. He extended his arm, which she took, and the two of them marched out of the Moth & Moon and up towards her cottage.

Mr. Reed stood in the doorway of the inn with his hands on his hips and his ever-present towel over his left shoulder. He sighed heavily and fixed his soft silvery hair into place as he surveyed the wreckage, both indoors and out. It would take days to clear up the mess left behind by the storm and by the villagers. He hadn't gotten much sleep. His private quarters were up four flights of stairs, and consisted of a bedroom, bathroom, and modest living room, which had been given over to some of the villagers he was friendly with, though his bed had remained his own. Even still, he only managed a couple of hours sleep. Between the noise of the storm, the noise of the crowd downstairs, and the noise from the numerous amorous adventures taking place in the small rooms upstairs, it wasn't exactly a restful night for anyone. He wondered how many new faces might be found in the village nine months from now.

He'd been raised in those quarters. Lived there with his parents and sister. She had gone to Blackrabbit Island when she was old enough to make her fortune, or so she had said. He received a letter from her every once in a while. She was doing well enough, had married a man and together they'd opened an ale house in the city. He couldn't imagine why. She'd run away from Merryapple precisely to avoid working in the inn. Why would she go and open one herself? He didn't understand. But she was happy, and that was what mattered. He'd only managed to visit her a handful of times over the years. She refused to come back to Blashy Cove, perhaps fearing the ghosts of her parents would rise from their graves and chain her to the stove in the tavern's subterranean kitchens. It was difficult for him to get away from the inn for too long, and he didn't care much for Blackrabbit Island or its people. Eva Wolfe-Chase had proved to be the surprising exception to this rule. A visitor from the mainland might not see too much difference between the islands, but their rivalry stretched back generations.

There were only a handful of people left in the tavern. The toymaker sat chatting with the paint shop owner's wife by the fireplace, and the Caddys were stuffing their belongings into some burlap sacks. Some chatter from the gallery upstairs told him others were still milling about up there.

Every surface had some combination of empty tankards, spillages, plates, and leftovers. It simply hadn't been possible for himself or his staff to keep on top of clearing up everything as the night wore on. He would have dearly loved to lock the doors for the next day or two and get the place back in proper order, but he knew there had been a great deal of damage to the village, and the inn had to remain open to serve as a hub for those affected, and for those trying to help. Lady Wolfe-Chase had helped him to appreciate something he'd always known, deep down—the importance of the Moth & Moon to the community. Sometimes, it helps to see our life through a stranger's eyes, he thought.

He took the towel from his shoulder and began to mop up a spillage of wine from one of the robust wooden tables when he became aware again of a fluttering at the corner of his eye. Spinning around, he finally found the source of it. He thought it might turn out to be a large wasp or maybe a bee, but as the sunlight caught its iridescent azure wings, he gasped. Fluttering past him was the largest blue moth he'd ever seen. Just like the ones he remembered from his childhood, the ones he'd chased through the long grass on the north coast of the island. The ones he'd thought long gone.

Mr. Reed held out his hand and smiled as the moth gently landed on his finger. He turned his hand slowly from side to side, admiring his unexpected visitor from every angle. The moth gently flexed its wings. Trimmed in white and dazzling blue on top, underneath they faded to grey with black spots.

"So, you're the one I've been chasing around all night," he said softly.

He thought about how he was going to display his latest find. This one deserved a case all of his own. Something special. Cedarwood, maybe? Or oak? But something stopped him. Instead of catching the moth in his hands, he simply stood there and admired it for a while, and then he carefully walked outside and went a few steps into the courtyard. Avoiding the fallen branches and other bits of debris, he stopped and held his hand up to the sky.

"Off you pop," he said, and with that, the moth spread its elegant wings and took flight, heading at first toward the sea, then banking and aiming itself towards the hills to the north.

And Mr. Reed kept smiling.

Chapter Nineteen

WHEN ROBIN AND Morwenna arrived at her cottage, they found the roof had been almost completely destroyed. Some of her belongings, which had been stored in the attic, had been strewn around neighbouring gardens, along with paintings she didn't have room to display. Among them were some unfinished pieces, including preliminary canvas sketches of the portrait of her and her husband. Robin held her hand as they entered the cottage, prepared for the worst. Mercifully, the painting still hung above her fireplace. With one hand she touched her chest and with the other the frame, and laughed a nervous little laugh. Robin left her alone with her thoughts and went back outside. Neighbours who had suffered less damage and were pitching in to help recover her possessions. There were several large trunks filled with old clothes, books, and letters. Some had burst open, and the items within had been soaked. As Robin was tidying up the contents of a large oak trunk, he dropped an old satchel onto the ground. It flopped open and something slid out. A small, leather journal, the colour of blood. As he bent down to retrieve it, he heard Morwenna call to him to leave it.

"Don't you worry about that, I'll get it," she said as she began to stoop down.

But Robin had reached it first. He lifted the item and studied it, turning it over in his hands. A single piece of soft, burgundy-coloured leather, folded over on itself and held closed with thin leather thong, at the end of which hung a brass pendant. This was shaped like a ship's wheel and decorated with nine tiny flowers on either side. The cover was embossed with a lavish compass design and the spine featured two X shapes formed by more strips of leather which held the pages in place. Lastly, another ribbon of leather was attached at the top as a sort of bookmark. A second pendant hung from it, in the shape of an anchor with a piece of rope wound tightly around it, a rope which emerged from a spindle centred in the crown of the anchor. This anchor pendant was exactly the same as the one sewn to Robin's own cap—the cap which had once belonged to his father.

He had recognised the notebook straight away, for he passed by it every morning on his way downstairs in his tall, thin house. This was the very same book that appeared in the portrait hanging in his landing, the portrait of his father. He remembered seeing his father writing in it many times when he was a boy. He always had it with him. Robin undid the strap holding the journal closed and opened the notebook to the first page, which read, in beautiful flowing script, "The Journal of Erasmus Shipp."

"Morwenner," he said, turning to face her. "This is Dad's journal."

Morwenna had turned pale as a sheet. Her mouth hung open.

"Why do you 'ave this?" he asked.

He felt confused, betrayed, even. She began to wobble and steadied herself with her cane.

"I thought 'e took it with 'im when 'e left. Why is it 'ere?"

Morwenna reached out for the journal. "It's just something to remember him by. Give it here."

He flicked through the pages. One word occurred over and over again. *Morwenna.*

"Why were you 'iding this?" Robin demanded. The friendly tone from his gruff voice had vanished. He was weary and ached all over and was in no mood for games.

"Please, Robin, it's nothing. Just give it to me," Morwenna wailed.

"It's not nothin'—it's my dad's journal, and you've 'ad it 'idden for over forty years!" he roared.

He was reading it now, the last entry, the day Erasmus Shipp signed on to a whaling vessel that was docked in the bay, the day he left his hastily scribbled will for Robin to find on the kitchen table. The entry read—in hurried, rushed script quite different from the elegant calligraphy of the first page—"I hope you can forgive us both."

"Forgive? Forgive who? You and Dad? For what?" he asked.

The raised voices had drawn a crowd. Duncan had arrived, carrying little Bramble, along with Louisa and May. Edwin was there with his parents, as were many of the other villagers. Some light raindrops started drizzling out of the remaining clouds.

Morwenna shook and shook. She didn't look at Robin.

"Please, Robin, not like this—I wanted to tell you—I wanted to talk to you, I said earlier..."

"Forgive you for what, Morwenner?" he boomed, shaking the journal at her. He'd never felt this kind of anger before. His face was warm, his stomach sick. He frightened himself with the tone in his voice. He sounded just like his father.

"For lying to you," she whispered. "I got to your house early that morning, the morning Erasmus left. I was looking for Barnabas. He hadn't been home all night. I thought Erasmus might know where he was. I saw the journal and his will on the kitchen table. He wanted to explain everything to you; he wanted you to know everything, in case he never returned. I think he knew he wouldn't be coming back."

Robin was motionless; a massive, bulky statue, frozen in the sodden garden. "What do you mean, explain everythin'? Explain what, exactly?"

"Your father and I were close, Robin. Very close. I loved my husband, but Erasmus and I had known each other since we were children, we had a...a bond that went beyond friendship. One evening, we were out on *Bucca's Call*. He was thinking of leaving the Cove for good. I was trying to convince him to stay. It was then I felt something, a pain not like any I'd felt before. I fell to the deck and...I gave birth. Right there and then."

A startled gasp came from the assembled crowd. Everyone knew Barnabas and Morwenna had never had any children. Standing at the front of the crowd, Sylvia Farriner had a very different reaction. While everyone else whispered and gasped in shock, she just sneered. Scowling at Morwenna, she hugged her shawl tightly around herself.

"I didn't know what to do; I didn't even know I was pregnant. I lay there on that boat, holding this tiny, beautiful baby. I couldn't tell Barnabas; he wasn't able to have any children; it would have destroyed him to know what I'd...what I'd..."

Morwenna's tears burst forth and someone from the crowd moved to comfort her, but Robin held out one hand to stop them. In the other, he still gripped the journal. He never took his eyes off Morwenna. She sobbed and sobbed, and Robin never spoke a word.

"We were out in the bay. No one heard the baby crying. We concocted some story about one of his hussies leaving a baby in his boat in the middle of the night. A woman he called Rose. Everyone believed him; he certainly had the reputation for it. It wasn't so far-fetched that some poor waif he'd courted had ended up pregnant. We knew there would be plenty of witnesses when the baby was discovered in the morning; he just had to act surprised. No one could ever know the truth. I couldn't do that to Barnabas, but I couldn't bear to be apart from my baby, either. So I offered my help to him, our help, to look after the child, help him raise him, take care of him when Erasmus was at sea, or whenever he needed. Barnabas...Barnabas was very supportive. He and your father were very close, the best of friends, really. He knew how much I had wanted children. Sometimes I wonder if...if he knew. Deep down."

Morwenna looked at Robin now for some glimmer of pity or understanding. He offered none.

"I took the journal and hid it. I couldn't face you knowing the truth. I tried to tell you so many times. I tried to say the words, but I just...couldn't." She sobbed again. Deep, mournful cries, decades in the making.

Robin felt the world rock beneath his feet. It was as though he was standing on *Bucca's Call*, swaying from side to side, up and down, in the crests and troughs of mighty waves. He looked at the small old woman in front of him, the woman who had raised him and loved him. The woman who had lied to him and deceived him. He lowered his head, turned his back, and walked away.

Morwenna stood alone, still quivering. Pulling at her shawl as if to hide her face, she staggered away from the on-looking crowd, towards the hills. Before long, the moss-covered woods were in sight. The narrow laneway was soaking wet and muddy. Her cane tapped on the stones as she hobbled along under the dripping boughs. Every few yards, a great trickle would splash her bonnet and cause her to flinch, but she held the bow of it tightly around her throat and hurried on, fuelled by something akin to desperation or perhaps sorrow. The storm had brought down some of the lighter trees, and she carefully avoided any fallen—or falling—branches, as well as wreckage from the village deposited by the winds. The scent of petrichor and lichen was overwhelming and, on any other day, would have dragged her through her memories and calmed her mind, but today they had competition.

Eventually, she came upon the island's graveyard—a simple meadow set a little ways into the woodland. Flat and green and peppered with wildflowers, it had proved the perfect spot for the people of Merryapple to lay their loved ones to rest, in the shadow of a huge, ancient, thick-trunked yew tree standing in the centre of the pasture. The grave markers—simple stone blocks engraved with name and dates—were placed around the tree in ever-widening concentric circles. The closer one went to the trunk, the older and simpler the grave. Some families chose to have symbols of the old beliefs adorn these markers, and here and there were etched a Green Man with his face made of leaves or a bare-breasted mermaid. It was said the roots of the great tree worked their way into each grave, providing it with nourishment and turning death to life.

She walked to the far end of the meadow and stopped beneath the far-reaching branches of the very same walnut tree where Erasmus had built his boyhood treehouse. There, she laid her hand on a granite slab engraved with his anchor symbol. The inscription beneath read *In Memory of Erasmus Shipp. 1700—1740. Lost at sea.* Morwenna had insisted the marker be placed in the graveyard, even without a body to bury. This had proved to be a controversial decision, given the circumstances surrounding his death, but at the time, everyone agreed little Robin deserved a place to remember his father. The gravestone was set far from the roots of the yew tree—the villagers had insisted on that much. They might not have believed in the literal truth of this tradition, but the symbolism was still important—body or no, there would be no life after death for this man. Morwenna's husband was buried on the opposite side of the graveyard, hidden from view by the trunk, as far from his murderer as possible.

From there, water dripping from the trees made it sound as though the rain had returned. She stood there for some time with her eyes closed and her hands resting on her cane, and listened.

Chapter Twenty

ROBIN WALKED PAST the Moth & Moon, lost in thought. His first instinct upon hearing Morwenna's confession had been to race to the harbour and cast off in *Bucca's Call*, to get away onto the sea, to find some peace, some space to think. Poor *Bucca's Call*. How he longed to sail in her.

A small group of men had gathered in the courtyard of the inn, preparing to mount a search for Jim and Allister Stillpond. Most of the village's sailors had been up all night drinking and were in no fit state to do so much as walk to the boat, let alone sail it on rough waters. Though the hurricane had passed, the sea was still quite turbulent and the light rain was turning heavy once again. Mr. Bounsell and Mr. Penny were organising the effort and had roped in Archibald Kind to help. Mr. Blackwall had also been press-ganged.

Seizing the chance to be of some assistance, Robin immediately volunteered to accompany them. He also helpfully offered the services of Edwin and Duncan, who were sent for.

The rescue party piled into the largest lugger that was still seaworthy. Not a single boat had escaped with their sails intact, so they rowed their way out of the bay, two men per oar, with Duncan acting as navigator. Mr. Blackwall had slipped on a pair of leather gloves and was gripping the oar very lightly, complaining loudly about what the grimy wooden seat was doing to the back of his immaculate breeches. Seawater that had been blown into the boat during the storm sloshed about the men's boots, and he made sure everyone was aware of what it was doing to his shiny shoe buckles. No one offered him any sympathy. Archibald Kind gave up rowing after about ten minutes but still went through the motions, letting the brawny Mr. Penny do all the work. This was spotted by Robin, who was sitting directly behind him.

"Pick up the slack there, Mr. Kind," he bellowed, in an unusually serious manner.

Archibald tutted and began rowing again.

"This is no place for a man like me." He sighed. "My talents would be best utilised in comforting the many women who've been left traumatised after the storm. Think of them, Mr. Shipp! They've lost so much—they need a strong shoulder to cry on!"

Mr. Penny turned and snarled at him. The gnarled sailor's wet, straggly hair hung like rats' tails from beneath his weather-beaten tricorne cap. He had a rough, stubbly, and unbalanced face, with a large scar running from his brow, across his milky left eye, and down to his jaw. Raindrops ran along this furrow as if determined to emphasise it. Archibald Kind started to row harder.

Rumbullion Bay was located in the larger of the small islets lying southeast of Merryapple. These islands were uninhabited save for scores of cormorants that made their nests in the cliffs. Caves riddled the little islet—a honeycombed labyrinth that made it the perfect hiding place for smugglers' loot and gave rise to more than a few stories of hidden pirate treasure. Only the most adventurous of Merryapple's residents ever visited those caves, however. Aside from the fact the isle was usually shrouded in mist, there was only one entrance large enough to moor at, and even this was narrow and lined with jagged rocks. Usually, a visitor would take a rowboat inside the mouth of the cave. The rescue party had no such luxury, but they did have the foresight to tie a tiny raft to the lugger and trail it behind them. This would be big enough for a search party and to carry out any bodies, if it came to that.

When the lugger approached the mouth of the cave, they saw no sign of the Stillpond's vessel.

"Are we sure this is where they are?" asked Mr. Penny.

"It's the most likely spot. Jim Stillpond likes to fish in the waters round 'ere. If they moored at the mouth, their boat was probably wrecked during the 'urricane," said Robin.

"And if they didn't come here?"

Robin scanned the horizon. From there, he could see two more far smaller islets—just rocky outcrops, really—and behind him in the distance, sat Merryapple island.

"If they didn't come 'ere, then they're at the bottom o' the sea," he said grimly.

They anchored their boat and climbed on board the raft. This required kneeling, which Robin's aching joints weren't happy about and so he sat back on his heels, trying to ease the pressure on his knees. The men each took up a small oar and began paddling. The tiny craft bobbed up and down violently on the choppy waters. As they approached the dark entrance to the cave, they held their lanterns up. It was deathly quiet.

"Hullo?" Mr. Penny called out.

The silence was shattered by the cawing and flapping of hundreds of cormorants, which came rushing out of the cave all at once, disturbed by the sailor's call. The men ducked and held their caps tight to their heads while the birds passed by, their squeals and squawks echoing through the cave in a deafening crescendo until finally the last bird left the cave and joined the rest of its flock, nestled on the cliff faces.

The men continued their journey and called out to Jim and Allister as they went, their voices blending with the sound of dripping water, reverberating around the chamber. Each man carried a lantern, but the light from them was pale and not up to the task of illuminating the whole cave. They called out as they reached the sleek, flat beach on the far side of the cave. In reality, it was simply a smooth area of rock worn down by the lapping tide. There was a stalagmite jutting up from the edge serving as a mooring post. Robin and Mr. Bounsell had both been there before, and though it was some years before, they thought they knew the layout fairly well, so it was decided they would be best served by dividing into two teams. Edwin and Duncan would accompany Robin, while Mr. Penny and Mr. Kind would go with Mr. Bounsell. It wouldn't do to become lost in there.

"Mr. Blackwall, you stay 'ere and guard the raft. The sea is still rough and we can't risk losin' it, or we'll be stranded," Robin ordered.

If that did happen, they could probably swim back to the lugger, but depending on what condition Jim and Allister were in, that might not be an option. He didn't think the finicky fishmonger would be much use in the dark, grimy caves, in any case.

"What happens if the water starts to rise again?" Mr. Blackwall asked, looking to the mouth to the cave—a ragged white shard torn from the blackness.

"Try not to worry about it," Duncan said.

"That's right, you try not to worry about it," Mr. Penny snapped. "Try not to worry too much about the lapping, sloshing waters at yer feet. Try not to worry about how deep those waters might be. What might be under there, sleeping on the floor, submerged but stirring from all this noise we're making, getting ready to burst forth and grab ya." He stuck his arms out quickly and wriggled his fingers for effect, causing the nervous Mr. Blackwall to flinch. "Try not to picture yerself floating in that stygian pool with infinite darkness below ya and crushing stone above. Try not to worry about how yer only escape is a maze of tunnels bringing ya deeper and deeper into the rocks, a winding, confusing tangle of channels, where precipitous drops or tidal surges wait around every corner. In fact, you stay here and don't worry yourself about anything at all, Mr. Blackwall."

He walked away, laughing his scratchy, unsettling laugh while Ben Blackwall stood wide-eyed and shaking.

Upon hearing the makeup of the teams, Hamilton Bounsell quietly took Duncan to one side while the other men sorted through the equipment they would need to carry. They hadn't had much opportunity to talk since the storm had struck.

"Are you sure about this? I can get Mr. Penny to swap with you, if you like?" Hamilton offered.

Duncan glanced over at Robin and Edwin as they lifted ropes and lanterns from the raft and divided them amongst the two groups.

"It'll be fine—it's different now. We talked things over in the lighthouse. I'll tell you all about it later. But thanks for the offer, Ham," Duncan said as he lightly tapped his friend on the arm. He knew Mr. Bounsell disliked being called that, which was almost entirely the reason he said it.

The tunnels were still wet, and water dripped from every surface. The sea level had risen much farther than anyone had suspected. As they called and searched, they grew increasingly concerned. They had retreated quite far into the islet by now, and if Jim and his son hadn't gotten in there quickly enough, they would have been caught by the rising waters.

Duncan, Robin, and Edwin navigated their way as swiftly as possible through the eastern side of the caves. The tunnels were slick, salty, grimy channels that riddled the island. The party's candlelight vitalised the sickly green and grey colours and caused the walls to ebb and pulse. Edwin said it was like walking into the belly of a great beast—the monstrous arteries of a titan. Duncan lagged behind the two taller men, his squat legs finding it hard to keep pace. They walked ahead, probing the darkness, squeezing through the narrow confines of the tunnels, watching out for each other, warning about areas of unsafe footing and hazardous rock formations. Robin slipped abruptly and hit the ground with a hefty thump. Edwin, who had taken the lead, turned and laughed, then held out a hand. Robin grabbed it and Edwin heaved him to his feet. They stood together, face to face for the briefest of moments, lit only by the lantern light, and to his surprise, in that single moment, Duncan felt as though he were able to breathe again, for what seemed like the first time in years. Shaking his head and laughing softly, he let them walk on while he stood behind a notably phallic rock formation and relieved himself.

Robin and Edwin chatted as they walked. Mostly it was about their surroundings as Robin wasn't ready to discuss what had happened with Morwenna. Suddenly, he stopped and held up a finger to his lips.

"Shush!" he whispered abruptly.

He listened carefully, certain that he heard a voice calling out before realising it was just the other team coming out of a nearby tunnel. Both groups had arrived at the same place from different shafts—a huge chamber crowned with thousands of stalactites. The heart of the islet. Minerals and crystals in the walls caught the light from their lanterns and threw it back in dazzling shards. The area they walked on sloped gently upwards before dropping off to the water far below. The lapping waves at the bottom of the chasm echoed throughout the cavern.

As the men reached the lip of the ridge, they heard weak voices calling from below. Holding their lanterns as low as they could manage, they spotted the two fishermen clinging to a tiny ledge.

"Jim! Allister!" Robin called out. "Are you injured?"

"No" came the faint reply. "We're fine but we can't climb out."

Glad to see them both still alive, the men buckled down to getting them out of their predicament. The fishermen had been stuck there overnight, and between the cold, the hunger, and the shock, neither one had the strength to pull themselves up a rope. Someone would have to go and get them.

"I'll go," Robin said without hesitation.

He took a rope and began to wrap it around his prodigious girth.

"You absolutely will not," said Edwin.

"I can manage." He frowned.

Edwin grabbed the rope from Robin's hands and began tying it around his own waist.

"Even if you hadn't collapsed yesterday, do you really think your joints are up to the climb? You'd be better off up here as an anchor. Duncan and Mr. Bounsell, too. Where is Duncan, by the way?"

"I'm here, don't panic, I'm coming," Duncan said, as he emerged from a tunnel.

"Where 'ave you been?" Robin asked.

"I was peeing, if you must know. Now, what am I doing?"

"You're bein' an anchor with us two," Robin said, indicating to himself and Hamilton Bounsell.

"Why us?" Duncan asked.

"Yer all very...sturdy," said Mr. Penny.

Robin, Duncan, and Mr. Bounsell were all heavy-limbed and robust, and each unconsciously touched their own sizeable bellies. While Duncan was by far the lightest of the three, his gut was still more than ample. Robin moved close to Edwin and double-checked his knots.

"They're fine. You taught me well." Edwin smiled.

"Are you sure about this? We're very 'igh up," Robin whispered. He didn't want the other men to hear.

"I can manage. I have to. Besides, you'll be up here. I'm in safe hands," Edwin said softly.

Robin finished his checks and put his hands on Edwin's shoulders.

"Just don't look down," he said.

Mr. Penny stood, holding another rope out to Archibald Kind, who raised an eyebrow and cocked a hip.

"I hope you're not suggesting I go down there?" he scoffed.

Mr. Penny growled, shook his head, and began tying the rope around his own waist.

"You'd be no use anyway," he snarled, half under his breath. "You'd snap like a bleddy twig."

Archibald Kind fixed a stray lock of hair into place and smirked. "Quite right. Better to send a thick oak, instead."

They tied the ropes around some rocky outcrops. When the makeshift pulley system was in place, with Robin and Hamilton Bounsell acting as counterweights, Edwin and Mr. Penny lowered themselves down the slippery rock face. Duncan checked the ropes and made sure everything was as safe as possible, and then he and Archibald Kind took up the slack. Once over the edge, the lanterns tied to their waists bounced as the men descended. More than once, they lost their footing as their heavy boots slipped on the rocks, causing them to slam against the bluff.

When they reached the ledge, they each took one of the shivering fishermen on their backs. Luckily, both men were of slighter frame so it wouldn't be too much trouble for the solidly built rescuers to carry them back up. Once secured, they began the slow climb back up the cliff. The black waters far below noisily churned and gurgled, reminding them all of what awaited them should they fall. The water probably wasn't very deep, meaning there would be little to protect them from hitting the cave floor. A fall from the tiny ledge would be dangerous; a fall from the climb back up would be certain death.

The men up top pulled the ropes to help, but it was slow going. Mr. Penny reached the summit first, having taken the frailer, elderly Jim Stillpond on his back. Both men clambered away from the cliff face and lay on the ground for a moment, catching their breath. Hamilton Bounsell gave Jim some water from a sheepskin he had tied around his waist. The old man was badly shaken but otherwise unharmed.

Meanwhile, Edwin was still ascending. The added weight of Allister had slowed him down considerably. Suddenly, Duncan was shouting and pointing.

Edwin's rope was beginning to fray. His calm, steady pace suddenly increased. His hands grasped the line over and over, his boots scraped and slid across the rock face, finding purchase in even the narrowest of fissures. There was no time to untie Mr. Penny's rope and drop it down to Edwin.

"Faster, Edwin, faster!" Robin called.

As he approached the top, Robin held firm, both hands clutching the rope in his vice-like grip and feet planted into grooves in the ground. Duncan and Hamilton Bounsell reached out and took Allister by his forearms, heaving him to safety. Edwin had grabbed the slick rocks and was about to pull himself to safety when his hands and boots slipped, causing the rope to finally snap. Edwin plunged down the rock face, toward the seething waters below.

Time seemed to slow to a crawl for Robin as he called out and dived to the ground, grabbing blindly at the air. Everyone was shouting all at once, and their voices blended into a bewildering cacophony. Edwin's sleeve ripped open, clasped tightly in Robin's hand.

"I've got you, Edwin. I've got you," he said.

Edwin dangled over the edge, striking against the rocks. The lantern that had been secured around his waist had been knocked loose and it plummeted into the darkness below—a tumbling box of light, ultimately swallowed by the wet, lapping dark.

Edwin reached out with his free hand to grab Robin by the arm. Duncan and Hamilton Bounsell had taken Robin by the legs and waist while Mr. Penny and Mr. Kind reached over the edge to grab Edwin's shirtsleeves, and together, they all pulled him over the ridge to safety.

Robin and Edwin lay on their backs, panting heavily. Light from the group's lanterns danced around the chamber. Sweat sat on Edwin's brow, and there was an unfamiliar look in his eyes. Robin abruptly let out a nervous laugh.

"I told you I wouldn't let you fall, Mr. Farriner." He playfully slapped Edwin's shoulder and, scrambling to his feet, offered him a hand up. They stood facing each other, then leaned in and hugged for a long time, laughing and feeling grateful to be able to do so, before beginning their journey back through the tunnels to the raft.

Alone in the chamber, Duncan walked to the edge of the ridge and stared down into the darkness. Reaching into his coat pocket, he withdrew the small piece of yellowed paper he had kept tucked inside. Flipping it open, he read it again, for the thousandth time, tracing the childlike scrawl with his thumb.

"Duncan!" Robin's voice echoed from the tunnel. "You ready or are you peein' again?"

Duncan took a deep breath and scrunched the note into a ball, then dropped it over the edge, letting it fall away into the chasm.

"I'm coming now," he called back. "I'm ready."

It took a couple of trips on the little raft to get everyone back to the boat. Jim and Allister were shaken but would recover in time. They had blindly raced through the tunnels to escape the water and slipped over the ridge. It was incredibly fortunate they had landed on the little lip jutting out from the cliff face. Allister had landed first, breaking his father's fall and thankfully nothing else. Sometime in the night, their fishing vessel had been shattered to pieces against the rocks. They had worried that if that happened no one would know they were in the caves.

Robin was lost in his thoughts, adrift in the events of the past few hours. Talking with Duncan, almost losing Edwin, Morwenna's lie—it was all too much to take in. How could she? How could she lie to him like that? For his whole life? As a child, every time she comforted him through his nightmares—the ones where he was left alone on an island, the ones where he saw his father's face under the waves—she knew. Every time she helped him cope with running his tall, thin house, she knew. As an adult, every time he set off to the towns of Blackrabbit Island in search of Rose, she knew. Every time he spoke about what his mother might have been like, she knew. Every time she...every time. She was there every time. Every time he needed help. Every time he needed advice. Every time he needed his mother. She was there.

Every.

Single.

Time.

Edwin played with the frayed edges of the tear in his shirtsleeve, the place where Robin had grabbed him. He pushed his fingers through and wiggled them.

"You ripped my good shirt," he said playfully. "I'm telling your mum."

Robin suddenly laughed and laughed. It took everyone quite by surprise. He laughed until he shook, until he sobbed, until his cheeks were wet, until he began to lose his breath, until Edwin slid over and put his arm around his shoulders. Through the haze of tears, Robin had begun to see clearly.

"My mum," Robin repeated. "I've got a mum."

Chapter Twenty-One

AS THE RESCUE boat approached the harbour, picking its way through the floating debris, the band of men could see a small crowd had gathered at the pier. At the forefront was Mrs. Stillpond, crying into a linen handkerchief.

Archibald Kind jumped from his seat and perched himself at the prow of the vessel, triumphantly waving his purple silk scarf and cheering. "It's fine. I've got them! They're both fine! I found them in the cave!"

The crowd cheered at this news, and they jumped and waved back frantically. Mrs. Stillpond cried even harder now.

"Sit down, you idiot," Mr. Penny snapped. "Anyone would think you swam out to the cave and carried them home on your back."

Archibald flopped back into his seat. His extravagant periwinkle coat, though somewhat sodden from the drizzle and sea spray, still managed to flare out around him like an ostentatious aura. He primped and preened his ruffled collar and sleeves, then he took a small ivory comb from an inside pocket and ran it through his flowing locks a few times, making himself presentable for his audience before another sharp growl from Mr. Penny forced him to put it back in his pocket and pick up his oar.

"My dear Mr. Penny, it is important, on occasions such as this, to look as marvellous as the actions one has undertaken. The people expect nothing less," Archibald said as he jutted his chin upward.

He wanted to make sure the villagers with the best eyesight were treated to his impeccable jawline as early as possible. They docked the craft at the pier, close to the shoreline, and disembarked. Archibald Kind was the first off, naturally, and he instantly began regaling the crowd with the heroic tale. He knew the importance of getting one's side of the story across first. Everyone else's account would simply be an interpretation—his would be the original.

The crowd helped Jim and Allister Stillpond up the slippery steps.

"Thank you, Mr. Kind, thank you so much," Mrs. Stillpond cried as she hugged Archibald, then her husband, then her son, and then Archibald again.

"Oh, it was nothing, Mrs. Stillpond. I was happy to help them," he replied, beaming his immaculate smile at the crowd.

"You what?" Mr. Penny barked. "We had to search every corner of the Moth & Moon and practically drag you away from that new barmaid. You had no bleddy intention of..."

"It doesn't really matter who done what." Robin Shipp interrupted, "All that matters is Jim an' Allister are safe, wouldn't you agree?"

"If you say so," replied Mr. Penny with a grin. "By the way, Mr. Kind, I think you left yer comb in the boat."

Archibald turned and immediately ran over to where the scarred sailor was standing.

"Did I? That's not like me. I don't see it," he said.

"Have a closer look," growled Mr. Penny as he slapped Archibald on his back and sent him crashing into the freezing cold water below. He landed with a terrific splash and floundered about, thrashing his arms and legs wildly while the crowd pointed and laughed.

"Help!" Archibald gasped. "Help!"

Robin Shipp cupped his hands around his mouth and bellowed, "Stand up, Mr. Kind!"

With that, Archibald relaxed and realised he was in shallow water. His boots touched the stony seabed and he scrambled to his feet. The waves lapped around his chest and no higher. His hair, once so bouncy and free, was now matted to his skull, and his elegant frilly shirt and coat clung to him like wet rags.

The tiny, frail form of Mrs. Hanniti Kind pushed her way to the front of the laughing crowd. Seeing her nephew standing like a drowned rat, she turned and stared up at the coriaceous Mr. Penny from beneath her bonnet.

"He slipped," coughed Mr. Penny before taking his leave.

Morwenna had returned from the cemetery and waited nervously to welcome the rescue party back to shore. Robin walked the short distance to her, and they stood there while people milled around them in chattering clumps. She braced herself, uncertain of what would come next. The last time she'd seen him, he'd formed a frightening silhouette against a brooding sky, more angry than she had ever seen him. What would he say now? What would he do?

She flinched when Robin knelt down and threw his enormous arms around her.

"You've lived with this secret so long," he said. "You waited all this time and you couldn't tell me. I understand, Mum. I understand."

And for the first time in her life, Morwenna Whitewater held her beloved son in her arms for all the world to see.

Robin walked back to the Moth & Moon with Morwenna hugging his waist as best she could. The assembled crowd followed them to get out of the rain, all the while discussing the details of what had happened to Jim and Allister during their time in the cave. Once indoors, Robin stood by the inglenook and relayed his version of events. Morwenna's tweed knights joined her at the round table, but this time, Mrs. Greenaway attempted to take Morwenna's traditional spot by the fireplace, only to be shooed away by the widow's cane. The knights listened to Robin's story and muttered amongst themselves, eyeing both him and Morwenna with suspicion. Robin, not usually one to pick up on such subtleties, couldn't help but see how they were behaving. Something had definitely changed. He sat down and sank into himself when he realised the cause—rather than Morwenna's standing in the community raising him up, it seemed he was dragging her down. He had thought all that was behind him, thought the village had started to embrace him, at last, but now he wondered if their suspicion of him would always remain.

As the day wore on, people began to gather at the inn, and it was once again bustling. Edwin sat at the table next to Morwenna with Robin, Duncan, and Hamilton Bounsell, and they were soon joined by the Ladies Wolfe-Chase. Toward sunset, the crowd was parted by the imposing frame of Mr. Wolfe, the blacksmith. He was garbed in his work clothes—a grey woollen waistcoat over a white linen shirt with the sleeves rolled up to reveal his powerful forearms. A leather apron was tied round his waist, in the pocket of which were stowed a well-used tongs and chisel. Every piece of clothing was flecked with soot and singed around the edges. His short, dark beard often caught embers from the fires and so had an uneven quality to it, with craters where the cinders had burned away the hair. He had deep-set eyes that were black as coal. In his hand, he carried a small, soiled painting.

He passed by his niece and her wife and quickly said hello; then he handed the painting over to Morwenna.

"I found this behind my forge," he said in his deep but surprisingly soft, warm voice. "It must have been blown there during the hurricane. I suppose there're bits and pieces all across the village."

"Oh, thank you very much!" said Morwenna, wiping the mud and soot from the small canvas.

The painting showed a handsome young man with flowing locks, a devilish smile, and wearing a faded-green crushed-velvet jacket with silver buttons.

"My Barnabas. He painted this a few months before he died."

She turned the painting round to let the group see. When she showed it to Robin's table, Edwin turned ashen. Without saying a word, he jumped to his feet, spilling several drinks. He glared at his mother across the room.

"Edwin?" Robin put his hand on the baker's arm. "What is it? What's wrong?"

Edwin didn't respond. He didn't even look in Robin's direction. He simply darted through the crowd and out of the Moth & Moon, pursued by his mother.

"Edwin?" she cried. "Edwin, stop. Whatever is the matter?"

He didn't answer. Instead, he ran away from the inn, in the direction of her house. His parents hadn't yet found time to begin repairs to their home. The shutters had been ripped from the walls, and every window had been smashed. Half the tiles from the roof had been blown off, and some of them lay in pieces all around.

Ignoring the damage, he ran upstairs and into the bedroom and began tearing through the wardrobe, causing clothes to fly everywhere, landing in heaps were they may. The room was covered in shards of glass and leaves, blown in by the storm. The remaining curtains had been shredded and flapped mournfully out of the empty window panes, like tattered arms outstretched for lost loves.

"Stop that at once. What are you doing?" his mother demanded.

And stop he did, once he found what he was looking for. Unable to speak, he simply glowered at her, making her back away from him.

Upon returning to the Moth & Moon, Edwin barged through the crowd. He marched right up to Morwenna, who was still sitting with the painting.

"Do you recognise this?" he asked, thrusting a garment into the old woman's hands.

She held the jacket for a moment, running her bent, wrinkled fingers across its faded emerald surface.

"Where did you get this?" she whispered.

"That's mine. Give it back!" his mother shrieked as she tried to tear it from Morwenna's hands.

His father must have seen them return and now held his mother back while Robin loosened her grip on the jacket.

"Mr. Farriner, where did you find this?" Morwenna asked.

"In my mother's wardrobe. It's been there for as long as I can remember."

His mother stopped struggling. She turned on the assembled crowd, her expression savage and lips twisted into a snarl. The whole tavern was watching and listening now.

"Why do you have my husband's jacket, Sylvia?" Morwenna asked. "My husband's favourite jacket?"

"I picked it up after his father dropped it!" she cried, pointing to Robin. "I was on the headland that night. I saw them arguing. I saw Erasmus Shipp push Barnabas Whitewater to his death!"

The crowd gasped and murmured amongst themselves.

"That's a lie," Robin said, jumping to his feet.

"I'd expect nothing less from a pirate," said Mrs. Greenaway in her haughtiest tone of voice.

"A pirate? What do you mean, a pirate?" Mr. Reed asked. "I won't have you throwing accusations like that around in my pub, Sylvia Farriner."

"Oh, but it's not an accusation, is it, Mr. Shipp? Is it, Lady Wolfe-Chase?" his mother snarled.

Eva Wolfe-Chase stepped forward into the circle that had unconsciously formed around the scene. She held her head high and clenched her fists tight. A lady she might be, but fight she most certainly could. Knowledge wasn't the only thing seamen respected; she'd had to learn how to handle herself as well.

"I heard you talking. Captain Erasmus Shipp was nothing more than a vicious pirate!" she roared.

"Mrs. Whitewater, is this true?" Mr. Reed asked.

Morwenna nodded. "He wrote about it in his journal. He captained a pirate boat he named the *Fledgling Crow*."

The look on Robin's face made it clear that she'd never revealed that before. While the crowd yelled and jostled, Eva strode into the centre of the breach, and quelled the crowd with nothing more than a tilt of her regal head and an icy stare.

"In 1726," she called out, "a ship came to attack Blashy Cove. It was repelled by three vessels. Does anyone here remember that battle?"

A murmur rippled through the crowd.

"Everyone who was here at the time remembers it. The Battle in the Bay, we call it," said Mr. Reed, still leaning on the bar. "It was the closest we ever came to being attacked by pirates. One of your father's boats was sunk, wasn't it?"

"That's correct," Eva replied. "The confrontation is mentioned in my father's records. The attacking ship was captained by a ruthless man named Thomas Oughterlauney. He was intercepted by two Chase Trading Company boats and one other."

"Another pirate vessel, if you believe the stories," said Mr. Reed.

"That's exactly what it was. Oughterlauney attacked and sank one of my father's ships. The other had no choice but to break off the assault and rescue the drowning crew. The rival pirate ship damaged Oughterlauney's vessel and pursued it out of the bay. That ship is mentioned by name in the company logs." Eva turned to face Morwenna. "It was called the *Fledgling Crow*."

Tuts and shouts of disbelief erupted from the older generation. The crowd had grown so loud that one could easily be forgiven for thinking the storm had returned.

"Giss on! What do you take us for?!" someone called from the balcony above.

"It's true, I swear it!" Eva shouted, quieting the crowd once again. "Once the harbour is back up and running, I will send for the records and you can read them for yourselves. Don't you see? Captain Erasmus Shipp saved this village from being sacked by pirates."

The tone and flow of the villagers shifted. Those who were there, who had witnessed the battle first-hand, struggled to remember the details, trying to marry this new insight to what they knew. Edwin's mother looked unhappy at this change of the crowd's mood and stepped into the fore once again.

"He killed Barnabas Whitewater!" she bawled.

Gobs of hot saliva flew from the corners of her mouth like a rabid animal. The crowd was turning on itself now. Some of them—mostly the elder portion , the ones who had been alive when Barnabas Whitewater died—had been siding with his mother, while the rest—the ones who had grown up with or after Robin—were siding against her. With the revelation Captain Shipp might have saved their lives, some of them found their convictions falter. Nonetheless, the shouting and banging of fists on tables and feet on floors was growing louder, yet still that instinctive circle remained.

"Captain Shipp reached out and brave Barnabas struggled," his mother screeched, spinning around with her arms spread wide, her shawl hanging from her limbs like ragged batwings, clearly revelling in the audience, in the attention, in the spite. "Erasmus Shipp had him by the arm. His coat came loose, and he stumbled back and fell. Fell to his death!"

The crowd roared again at this. Barnabas Whitewater had been well loved and his death had rocked the island. Decades of pent-up anger and resentment was beginning to spill out.

"Wait, WAIT!" Edwin roared at the top of lungs.

No one had ever heard the baker raise his voice before, and the volume and weight of his bark stunned them into silence. Edwin faced his mother now. "Did he stumble, or did Captain Shipp push him?" he asked quietly.

"He was pushed! He...he... Erasmus had him by the arm, they were fighting, yelling, Barnabas—beautiful, sweet Barnabas—he was putting on his jacket, he twisted, turned, tried to break free and he...he fell. He fell onto the rocks."

The crowd was silent now, and the circle tightened. She looked trapped. She shrank into herself, becoming crouched; her red hair manifestly more wild and untamed than usual.

"Erasmus ran; he dropped the coat; he ran right past me. I was hiding behind the Wishing Tree—he never even knew I was there. I took the coat. It was his; it was Barnabas's. It was all I had left of him."

His father approached her.

"Sylvia? What do you mean it was all you had left?" he asked her quietly. "What was Barnabas to you?"

"I loved him. I loved him more than she ever could." Pointing now to Morwenna, who sat shaking in her seat. "But he wouldn't even look at me—I was too young for him. He only had eyes for her. So I had to settle for you." She nodded towards her beleaguered husband, the casual venom in her voice confirming what everyone had always suspected. She'd never loved him. Not really.

"Why did you never say anythin' about this?" Robin asked.

"Why would I? To ease your mind? Or hers?" she said, pacing towards Morwenna.

The crowd were on edge now, and Eva looked poised and ready to pounce on his mother if she attempted to strike Morwenna.

"The man I loved was dead. And now I know why. It was because of her. Erasmus must have told Barnabas she was your mother. That's why they were fighting. That's what caused him to fall. Then Erasmus ran away, ran back to his pirate brethren. It was justice that his boat sank. Justice that dragged your father to the bottom of the sea."

She spat the words out of her cruel, twisted mouth like lumps of gristle. She had stopped pacing now and drew herself to her full height, lifting her chin and narrowing her gaze.

"I'm glad I never said anything," she hissed at Morwenna. "I'm glad you suffered."

Edwin stared at his mother in shock and disbelief. Silently, his father pushed his way through the crowd and left the building.

The people had fallen deathly silent, in particular, the elders of the village—Morwenna's contemporaries. All this time, they'd said Captain Erasmus Shipp was a murderer and taken their vengeance out on his son. They passed their sentence and handed Robin's punishment down the generations for their own children to administer. Edwin stared at Mrs. Greenaway, who was covering her mouth with her hand. She'd been twisted and turned and manipulated by his mother's words. She—like all of them—had decried Robin, called him a menace, nothing more than the progeny of a killer, when in truth he'd never been anything other than kind and pleasant to each of them. One by one, the older folk of the village turned to each other.

"He fell," they repeated.

"He fell."

When he reached his house, Nathanial Farriner walked calmly through the shattered glass, dank leaves, and branches, and went upstairs. He fetched two large wooden boxes and quietly filled them with his wife's clothes and belongings. Then he lifted them downstairs and placed them on the wet path outside, one by one.

Shortly afterwards, his wife returned, escorted by a visibly upset Edwin. Sylvia was unusually quiet. They stopped outside, and she pointed at the boxes on the ground, confused. Her clothes were stuffed haphazardly inside, leaves and glass mixed among them. Nathaniel hadn't bothered to remove them from her garments before packing them. Water dripped onto them from the guttering overhead.

"What's this?" she asked.

Nathanial stood in the doorway of their home, his arms folded.

"You have to leave. The village. I don't care where you go, but you can't stay here."

He had expected her to scream, to argue, to fight with the same ferocity she had shown earlier. Instead, she simply snorted derisively. A half laugh of pure contempt. She said nothing. She simply turned and walked towards the harbour, leaving behind him, her son, and of all her belongings.

Chapter Twenty-Two

ROBIN'S KITCHEN WAS in a state of organised disarray. There hadn't been much time lately to worry about domestic chores. He washed out some cups and took the whistling kettle off the hob. After excavating his chipped ceramic teapot from under a pile of plates, he warmed it with a little water from the kettle and added some tea leaves. The pot was white and decorated with an idyllic farming scene. It had been in the house for as long as he could remember. He assumed his father had bought it, or perhaps it even belonged to his grandparents. He hadn't ever considered it before, but just recently, he found himself thinking a lot more about his past in general and his father in particular.

He kept his father's journal on the pile of books by his bedside and read a little more of it every chance he got. The very first entry simply read "Captain Jonas Shipp died today" and was dated 15th May 1717, roughly four years after Erasmus and his father had left Blashy Cove for the first time. There were scores of entries—missives regarding life on board ship, copies of maps of unnamed islands, and other bits and bobs. There was a single page dated 7th June 1726 that simply read "Home." Thereafter the entries became more sporadic, with larger time gaps and fewer details. For the amount of times Robin remembered seeing his father with this journal, he had expected it to contain far more information. It wasn't until he reached the latter part that he discovered why Morwenna had kept it hidden all these years. The final entries were a letter. A letter to him, written by his father. A letter he was supposed to read.

1ˢᵗ July 1740

My name is Erasmus Shipp. I have had this journal for over twenty years, and used it to keep notes, copy maps, and mark important events. I am writing these following entries for my son,

Robin. There is much you need to be told, and I worry something may happen to me before you are old enough for me to talk to you, man to man.

I hope that someday you will read this.

I hope that you will understand.

I hope that you will forgive.

I was born in the village of Blashy Cove during the springtime of 1700. My father, Jonas Shipp, was a fisherman. My mother, Emily, was a seamstress. My earliest memory is of watching my father depart on a launch, heading towards a huge ship in the distance. I distinctly remember my mother with tears in her eyes, telling me to wave. I didn't see my father again for three years.

He worked on a whaling vessel, and over the course of my childhood, he spent more time at sea than at home. He was distant, in place and in heart. I was frightened of him for most of my life. The coldness of the sea seemed to have seeped into his bones, draining the love and warmth from him.

I spent most of my childhood terrorising the other children of Blashy Cove. Those I couldn't bully, I ignored. When I wasn't fishing from the edge of the pier or parading about in a little rowboat, I was in the woods on the west of the island. I had found one large tree in particular—a walnut tree overlooking the graveyard- up which I had dragged some planks of wood to lie across its thick branches. From this elevated platform, I shouted my orders to the other boys below. Only a chosen few were ever allowed to join me up there.

Despite the number of boys who palled around with me and the number of girls I kissed, there was only one person who I truly considered a friend. A short, dark-haired girl named Morwenna Day. She was born a few months after me, and our parents were friends. Or at least, our fathers drank together in the Moth & Moon and our mothers spoke at the market. She wasn't afraid of me. Or of anything else, for that matter. She dived off every rock the boys did, climbed the same trees, sailed in the same boats. She would never let me get away with anything. Called me stupid when I thought I was being clever. Laughed at me when I tried to impress her. Slapped me when I lied to her. She saw right through me. Right to the heart of me.

My mother tried to teach me how to read, but I was a slow learner, with little to no patience. It wouldn't be until years later that an old sailor named Mr. Howe would teach me how to read and write on board the ship that would be my home for many years.

It was a bright morning in the summertime of 1713 when my father told me I would be accompanying him on his next voyage at sea. He had spent most of that year, and the previous one, teaching me the proper way to fish in the cove. I had always been interested in this, and had picked up some knowledge and—according to him—some bad habits. My mother had already packed my belongings into a canvas bag. I was scared, Robin. Very scared. But I didn't show it. She handed me the bag and told me to open it. Inside—on top of my clothes—was a plain, navy-coloured peaked cap. She reached into the bag and lifted it out, picking a small piece of lint from the brim, then she placed it on my head and gave me a kiss on my cheek. The cap was too big, but she said I'd grow into it.

It was that very same cap which Robin wore every day, and he touched it reflexively.

Then both she and my father marched me out of our house and down the harbour. I saw the whaling vessel docked out past the lighthouse. How big it looked. How daunting. I boarded the little launch wordlessly, and watched as men with arms like tree trunks and faces like broken glass heaved the oars and pushed us through the calm waters. Despite the fear, I felt a sense of pride. My father trusted me enough to bring me with him. My mother was holding a handkerchief to her face, trying to force a smile as I waved farewell. I couldn't have known it then, of course, but this would be the last time I would ever see her.

Morwenna was there as well, but she didn't wave. She just stood and watched. None of the village boys came to see me off. I expect they didn't know I was going, but even if they did, I doubt they would have come. I expect they were glad to see the back of me.

The next few years were the toughest of my life. Nothing could have prepared me for life aboard a working whaling vessel. The roughness and desolation of the cold seas, the anger and violence of the sailors, the stench of whale meat. In Blashy Cove, I was top of the heap. On the boat, I was bottom of the pile. I scrubbed the decks—a particularly grim job after a successful whale hunt. I sharpened the harpoons. I assisted the cook, which basically meant chopping vegetables for hours upon hours. The only job I didn't mind was climbing the rigging. While I was nervous at first, my time spent in the trees at home had served me well. I skittered up and down those nets with natural ease. I was a fierce, pugnacious lad back then. Tough and callused from the many fights, falls, and failures of my earlier life, and built like my father—square, solid, and strong.

Roughly two years after leaving Blashy Cove, my father earned the rank of captain. Through some wrangling—the details of which I'm unfamiliar with to this day—the ship we served on became his property, and the previous captain departed. I suspect there was some gambling involved, despite there being a very strict code against games of chance on board. His tenure as captain was tumultuous, to say the least. The crew were wildly displeased at the change in command. We caught increasingly fewer whales, the money began to dry up, and the crew became even more disgruntled. Eventually, working on that ship became an untenable prospect and my father arranged for the boat to be sold, then he and I parted ways with the crew and the whaling business.

We were at some port I forget the name of—wherever it was, the sun bore down mercilessly during the day and the air smelled of jasmine at night—figuring out what to do next when my father was approached by a man in a very neat uniform and a very tall wig. They spoke in confidence, and I was never privy to the exact details, but the upshot is my father purchased a smaller ship— which I renamed the Fledgling Crow*—hired another crew, and suddenly we were privateers. It was our job to intercept pirate vessels on behalf of the authorities, capture—or kill—the crew, and seize any contraband.*

That word shocked him. "Kill." He'd spent his whole life refuting the idea that his father was a killer.

This was a very different way of life for us. It was also significantly more exciting. And dangerous. We had a successful couple of years, during which time I learned a great deal more about sailing, fighting, and being a captain. My father and I had a working relationship only. He was as cold and distant as ever, and I was less spirited than I had been in my youth.

After a few years of this work, we became aware of a distressing turn of events. It appeared having civilian vessels doing the work of the navy had become an embarrassment, and increasingly difficult to justify to the public. Any privateer vessel caught breaching their letter of marque—their licence, that is—in even the slightest way were immediately declared pirates and hunted down. And so it was in the spring of 1717 my father, myself, and the whole crew of the Fledgling Crow—*for a minor miscalculation in the reporting of a seizure of rum—were declared pirates. We were set upon by two navy vessels, which hunted us for weeks. We tried to explain how we had simply miscounted the amount of rum recovered, but they were convinced we had kept some for ourselves—either to drink or to sell—and that was good enough for them. There would be no hearing. No appeal.*

The next part is a blur. I remember a lot of gunpowder smoke in the air, the shouting of the men, the creak of the masts. One of the navy vessels was close to us, attempting to board. Buckshot from their muskets whizzed around our ears. I heard something slump to the deck behind me, and turned to see my father lying there, propped up against the ship's wheel, holding his throat. He gasped slightly a handful of times, and then he was gone. I assumed command and through sheer luck and a fortunate strike from our cannons, managed to evade our would-be captors.

In calmer waters, we buried our dead at sea. I said farewell to my father as he sank below the waves. I wish I could say I shed a tear, that I felt a great swell of grief, but the truth is I felt nothing. I was numb.

Robin re-read that passage several times. His father had never told him any details about what happened to his grandfather, saying simply that he'd died at sea. He felt a great swell of pity for his father. To feel so little at the loss of someone so important must be an odd sensation indeed.

My crew and I—for they were my crew now—spent a long time discussing what we would do next. We knew there was no chance of us returning to respectable work and decided if we were going to be treated as pirates, then we would act the part. We began raiding vessels, capturing goods which we used either to keep our supplies topped up or to sell at less reputable ports. We had a profitable few years. Other pirate crews set about crafting a reputation for themselves, a cloak of fear to drape about their shoulders in the hopes their targets would be so overcome with terror that they would make mistakes or be unwilling to fight at all. We took a different approach, eschewing the cultivation of notoriety and allowing our exploits to be attributed to the blowhards and glory hounds. Let them grab the attention of the pirate hunters and the navies; we were content to operate in obscurity.

There were times when a sailor's loyalty to his ship or masters would cloud his judgement and goad him into taking arms against us. Where we fought, it was only for a swift end, a decisive act to curtail any other thoughts of action from the crew.

He took comfort in the idea that perhaps his father hadn't been a bloodthirsty buccaneer after all, but fought only when necessary.

It was at one of the disreputable ports I mentioned where I made what I now realise was one of the worst mistakes of my life. It was 1723, and needing to bolster our numbers, we took on a handful of new crew members, including a man named Thomas Oughterlauney. Initially, he was sullen and withdrawn, but I was assured by his associates that he was a hard worker and reliable. This turned out to be true, in a sense. What they hadn't mentioned was how he was prone to extremely violent outbursts, and that he was ambitious. He quickly began spreading dissent among the crew. My men were loyal, but he turned some of their heads with talk of larger shares of our bounties. As we continued our raids, he became more and more violent, until one day he murdered a fellow crewman. A man named Anthony Cook. A good, loyal man who had served with my father and I since the very beginning.

Robin thought perhaps the man was related to old Oliver Cook, who lived in the north of Merryapple.

After that, I had no choice but to follow our code and maroon Oughterlauney on a remote island. I knew there was a source of fresh water and plenty of food. As was our way, I left him a musket with a single shot. He would live the rest of his days in isolation, or—if life became unbearable—he would use the musket.

I hoped that would be the end of the matter and I would hear no more of Mr. Oughterlauney, but it was not to be. He was rescued from the island and staged a mutiny on another vessel. We would eventually come to blows again in a decisive battle that would leave a sour taste in my mouth. The navy had long since given up on chasing us and I handed over command of the Fledgling Crow *to my most trusted crewmember, a man named Collan Kind. For the first time in over twelve years, I returned home to Blashy Cove.*

Mrs. Hannity Kind was prone to singing the praises of her brother, Collan, the brave sailor. Robin wondered how she'd react to the news that he was a pirate, too.

Upon landing at Merryapple pier, I went straight to my childhood home on Anchor Rise. Another row of houses had been built on the opposite side of the road. Indeed, there were a good deal more houses and buildings now than when I was a boy, they stretched up the hills and beyond. Despite the expansion, everything felt smaller than I remembered. I had left as an agile and energetic boy, and returned as a lead-footed and weary man. The growth of the village during the years I'd been away necessitated the addition of numbers to the houses on the Rise. My home was now number five.

I nervously knocked on my old front door, cap in hand, expecting my mother to answer. Instead, it was our neighbour, Mrs. Buddle. For a moment, I thought I'd come to the wrong house, perhaps they also had a sky-blue door and I'd become disorientated. After getting over her shock at seeing little Erasmus standing before her a full-grown man, she invited me in. She poured me some tea and we sat in the kitchen. The house was so quiet. So still. She talked on and on about nothing until finally I asked her where my mother was. I wanted so badly to speak to her, to hear her voice, to tell her what had happened to my father, to explain why I hadn't returned sooner. Mrs. Buddle welled up as she broke the news to me. Apparently, she had taken ill after receiving word of my father's death and been left for years in a weakened condition. She had passed away in the spring, a handful of months earlier. Assuming I would return one day, Mrs. Buddle and her husband had been looking after her home—my home— ever since.

As Mrs. Buddle left the house, closing the door behind her, I sat in the front room of my childhood home and realised that, for the first time in my life, I was completely and utterly alone. In my heart, I had always held this place as a safe port of call. My unchanging rock to which I could return at any time, finding my mother standing at the shore as she had done when I left, unaging, unbending, my true north. Alas, that was a childish notion, and I had returned to find nothing but an empty house. If I had come home sooner, perhaps I could have prevented my mother's passing, or at least spoken to her, one final time.

Regret is a horrible thing. Regret will eat you, Robin. It will burrow inside and gnaw at your very soul, if you let it.

He closed the journal and sat back in his chair, sniffing away a tear. After the events of the past few days, his father's words struck right to the heart of him. He walked to the window, composing himself, before returning to where he left off.

I found the village as I had left it—industrious and welcoming. The boys I had run around with had become men—some worked the sea, others the fields. The girls had become women, and most had married. Including Morwenna Day, or Morwenna Whitewater as she was by then. I saw her later that evening, standing by the harbour as the sun was setting, silhouetted against the burning orange sky. I recognised her instantly. She greeted me warmly, as if I'd only been gone a day. She introduced me to her husband, a charming fellow named Barnabas. They both made me feel very welcome as I tried to build a new life for myself on Merryapple.

I commissioned a lugger from the local shipbuilders. Together, we worked on the plans and crafted something a little different from the other boats of the harbour. I wanted to be able to comfortably operate alone, and thus she was built somewhat smaller than the average lugger. I named her Bucca's Call, *and she proved herself sturdy and reliable, and more than adequate for my needs.*

He felt a sharp pang of loss for his boat once again. She'd served both him and his father well.

At first, I began fishing for pilchards, but there were already plenty of other fishermen in the village doing this, so I decided instead to focus on oyster dredging. This proved to be much more successful, and profitable. I sold them to old Bob Blackwall, who ran the fishmongers in the village.

I began to feel lonely, and my thoughts returned to Morwenna. The three of us—her, Barnabas, and I—spent a lot of time together. I wanted to know what had happened while I was away. I wanted to reconnect, I suppose is the word. Reconnect with my home. With my past. They wanted to hear tales of seafaring adventure. We drank cider in the moonlight and swapped stories. Until the night I pushed it too far. Barnabas was painting, as he usually did, and Morwenna and I walked along the headland. We stopped under the Wishing Tree and I kissed her. She looked so shocked. I did it because I was drunk. And because I wanted to. I swore to myself I wouldn't lie to you, Robin. I'm not proud of my actions, but I did it and I'd do it again. I kissed her because I wanted to, plain and simple. She slapped me and ran away. I felt guilty. More guilty than I ever could have imagined. So, the next morning, I packed up Bucca's Call *and left Merryapple. I began touring the islands, sleeping with any woman who would have me. I was handsome enough, so I'm told. Tall, blonde, sturdy. I was also wealthy, which didn't hurt matters.*

"Modest, too," Robin said as he rolled his eyes.

I spent a lot of time on Blackrabbit. Drank a lot. Screwed a lot. I was determined to find some woman, any woman, to replace Morwenna in my heart. I found none.

Two years later, I returned once again to Blashy Cove. This time, I was determined to have her. The girl who got away. The girl I should have married. It would have been easier if Barnabas had treated her badly. If he'd disliked me or if I'd disliked him. But try as I might, I couldn't. He has a way of disarming people, a charming sort of naivety that gets under your skin. You can't help but like him. There were plenty of girls in the village who would regularly throw themselves at him, including a red-headed girl who still pesters him at every opportunity, but he only has eyes for Morwenna.

I'll spare you the details, Robin, but suffice it to say Morwenna eventually fell for my charms. We stole away together every chance we got. I still felt guilty, but this time, I stayed. I was getting what I thought I wanted.

Then one night in 1730, my whole world was changed. Morwenna and I were aboard Bucca's Call, out in the cove. We watched the falling stars overhead when suddenly she cried out. She was wracked with pain and I panicked. My time at sea hadn't prepared me for what was about to happen. She fell to the deck, screaming, and just a few minutes later, I was holding the tiny fragile body of my son in my arms. You were so small, Robin. We wrapped you up and wondered what we were going to do. Morwenna had no idea she was pregnant, and you were definitely mine. Barnabas was unable to father children. Everything was different now.

Between us, we concocted a story about a woman from Blackrabbit Island—who I named Rose—coming to Blashy Cove under the cover of darkness and leaving you in my boat. It was Morwenna who named you. She knew we had to pick a name that couldn't be tied to either of us, and she had always liked that one. It was roughly an hour before dawn when we got back to the harbour, left you safely in Bucca's Call, and returned home. When the sun rose, I would return to the harbour, ready to set sail for the day's fishing, as usual. It was the longest hour of my life. I worried about someone finding you first. I worried about you dying in the cold. Finally, the sun began to rise, and I tried not to look like I was hurrying to the harbour. Everything went exactly as we had planned. We "found" you on my boat, with the note I had written, and that was that. The whole village had seen me discover my son.

At first, he didn't know what to make of the notion that his father was prepared to run the risk of letting his newborn son freeze to death in order to save his own skin. But then he reasoned it wasn't really for his father's sake, but rather for Morwenna's and Barnabas's. In any case, he resolved not to dwell on it.

For the next few years, I devoted myself to you, Robin. With the help of Morwenna and Barnabas, I raised you and made sure you were able to take care of yourself. I worked hard as well. I had money left over from my pirating days, and I wanted to make sure you didn't end up like me or my father. I didn't want you to have to go to sea. I didn't want that coldness soaking into your bones. You were the happiest, most joyful baby any father could have wished for. There were several times when I had to leave you in Morwenna and Barnabas's care for extended periods. Events conspired to drag me back to sea. Either work I needed to take or unfinished business aboard the Fledgling Crow. *But the less said about that, the better.*

It was difficult for Morwenna; I realise that. We weren't lovers. We were something else. Secret parents. Barnabas knew we were close, and over time he and I had become dear friends, too. I love them both. It upsets me that we can never tell Barnabas the truth, but he is a sensitive soul, and we know how it would hurt him. There's nothing noble in this lie, Robin. I'm not trying to make excuses; I'm simply trying to be honest.

Please don't be angry with Morwenna for hiding this from you. I put her in an impossible position. And please don't tell Barnabas. I know I have no right to ask you, but telling him now would do no good. Let him live the rest of his days in peace.

Barnabas painted my portrait in the winter 1736. We sat by the fire in his house and talked for hours, the three of us. It took weeks. You were there for most of it. I'm sure you remember. He has such talent, that man. I thought some of it might rub off on you, but you showed little interest in art. You preferred to be on the water. So much like your father. Hopefully not too much.

I hope that I—that the three of us—gave you a good start in life.

9th August 1740

I have to put an end to this.
Please forgive me, Robin. You deserve better.
I hope you can forgive us both.

When Eva Wolfe-Chase had told Robin that his father was part of the crew of a pirate ship, Robin had scarcely been able to believe it. Hearing it from Morwenna made it real for him. Another secret she had kept from him. Robin had always maintained whatever happened to Barnabas on the headland hadn't been Erasmus's fault, and now the whole village knew that was true. What still troubled him, however, was what really happened before the sinking of the *Caldera*.

Chapter Twenty-Three

WHILE THE TEA brewed, Robin cleared a small tray and loaded it with two cups, saucers, and a little bent, tarnished spoon. He carried the tray into his living room where Morwenna was sitting by the simple stone fireplace. The room was small and bright and painted the same pale blue as most of the rest of the house. Its white floorboards were as much in need of a new coat of paint as the ones in Robin's bedroom. The living room was plainly furnished with a settee, which was old when his grandfather was young, and two armchairs. A glass-doored cabinet rested against one wall and was home to some trinkets from various voyages.

He'd inherited almost every piece of furniture from his father, who'd gotten it from his father. Robin never saw the sense in replacing anything unless it was damaged beyond repair. The armchairs, however, had been carved by Duncan. Robin thought many times about getting rid of them, but he told himself that was wasteful.

Morwenna seemed distant. Haunted. They hadn't spoken much since the scene in her garden a few days before. Things were different now. When Robin looked at her, he didn't just see the woman who had practically raised him; he saw all the years they'd wasted. All the time she hid from him, denied him. And that's what it felt like, no matter how much he understood her reasons why, he couldn't help it. He felt like she'd denied him. He loved her, and she knew that, but somehow it wasn't enough. It didn't mean enough. His love wasn't good enough. It wasn't right and it wasn't fair, but right then, it's how he felt.

"You don't know how hard it was," she said at last over the crackling from the fireplace. "Every day, knowing you were so close. I had to be so careful, couldn't let anyone know or even suspect. I acted as your nurse when I should have been your mother. The first time Erasmus went off to sea after you were born, you came to stay with Barnabas and me. You probably wouldn't remember—you were only about three years old.

Erasmus needed the money, I think. He didn't want to go, he agonised over the decision, leaving you for so long. He knew what it would mean, what it would do to me. He wanted a better life for you, didn't want you to have to go to sea for months or years at a time, not like he did, not unless it's what you wanted to do. And he did it, too. Over time, he provided for you, more than enough for your whole life."

"Some of it must 'ave been pirate money, though. And 'e said somethin' about havin' to go back to his old ship," Robin said.

"You read his letter, then? In the journal? I suppose it must have been for something more than just the money. Your father liked his secrets."

"'e weren't the only one," Robin said.

He might understand her reasons, but he still felt hurt. If Morwenna was wounded by this comment, she didn't show it.

"For the two months he was away, you lived with Barnabas and me, and we were like a little family. It was so hard when Erasmus returned and you went back home. So hard. I had to pretend to be happy, happy you were back with your father, but I cried every day for a week. I hid away while Barnabas was working, or took myself off to the Wishing Tree. Lying against it, you can't see the waves or the horizon. It seems as if the sky falls forever, as if the whole island is adrift among the clouds. I used to dream of sailing away with you and Barnabas. Or you and Erasmus. I couldn't tell Barnabas that I was sad. I couldn't even tell your father. It wouldn't have been fair. Barnabas doted on you, you know. Having a child in the house meant so much to him, to both of us."

"'E were always so kind to me," Robin said. "'E never got angry. 'E always looked after me. I remember bein' in your 'ouse almost as much as me own. Remember when 'e tried to teach me 'ow to paint? Showin' me 'ow to 'old a brush and that. I couldn't even paint a cloud. The patience o' that man! I never did get the 'ang of it, but some of my 'appiest memories are of watchin' 'im workin' on a canvas while you sat and made fishin' nets for the men—or baked or sewed. You said you should 'ave been my mother, but in every way that matters, you were. Don't you see, Morwenna? I were the luckiest boy in the world—growin' up, I 'ad a mother and two fathers."

She cried again. Heart-deep sobs that sounded as if they were dredged up from the darkest part of her soul. Robin handed her a handkerchief.

"Oh, Robin, he knew. He knew what I'd done. He died because he knew."

"You said before you always suspected that. Anyway, you can't be certain. Sylvia Farriner didn't 'ear what they were arguin' about. It could 'ave been anythin'."

"There's something else."

Robin braced himself. He wasn't sure he could handle any more secrets.

"What now?" he asked.

Morwenna pulled at the handkerchief, twisted it.

"The night your father left—the night Barnabas died. I met Erasmus and I told him we couldn't see each other anymore. Not in...*that* way."

Robin furrowed his brow and considered this. "You mean—you two were still seein' each other? All that time?"

Morwenna nodded while Robin stood up.

"But I thought... I assumed you'd stopped after I was born. Dad never said—in his letter, I mean— 'e never said anything about you two still seein' each other. Nothin' about it in the rest of the journal. I thought it would 'ave been too risky, what with you bein' 'ere so much. Spendin' so much time around Dad. Too obvious."

"We tried to stop. We did," Morwenna wailed. "And it's true that it wasn't the same anymore. What we had was different, but it was still... I don't know how to explain it, Robin. When Barnabas held my hand, my heart calmed. I was at peace. When Erasmus held my hand, my heart galloped. Neither one was better or worse than the other. Both felt right. Both felt like home."

"So, you told my dad you couldn't...be together anymore, and then 'e went and told Barnabas about you?"

Morwenna began to shake again. She nodded violently.

"He must have. I told him, and he was so angry. He couldn't understand why. Why after all this time. I told him it couldn't go on forever. It wasn't right."

"Is that what 'is last journal entry were about?" Robin asked. "The bit about putting an end to something?"

"No. At least, I don't think so, but when I saw his journal the next morning, those final few lines... Is it any wonder I hid it? How would it have looked to the village?"

She was shaking again and dabbed her eyes with a handkerchief. While she regained her composure, Robin poured some tea.

"What made you fall in love with my dad in the first place?" he asked suddenly. Morwenna was shaken by the question and took some time to consider her answer.

"He was wild," she said at last, still dabbing her eyes with Robin's handkerchief. "Like a force of nature. A hurricane. He blew through this village from the moment he could walk. Not an inch of it went unexplored by him. He climbed every tree in the woods, kissed every girl, sailed in every boat. We were the same age, and we palled about together, but we were never...you know. Together. We were friends, but that was all. He had too much of a roving eye to ever settle for me. He went off to sea when he was twelve, I think? Maybe thirteen. Young, anyway. Him and his dad, Jonas. Proud as could be, they both were."

"'E said 'e were scared. In 'is letter," Robin said. He still had trouble picturing his father as a young boy.

"I know, but he didn't show it. He never showed it. A few years later, I met Barnabas and we fell in love. We were so happy together. And then Erasmus came back alone. He'd grown so much. The wildness was gone, he was quieter. Focused. Something had happened to his father, but he would never tell me what it was. He was just gone. As he tried to settle down in the village he'd left as a boy and returned to as a man, we spent a lot of time together.

"It's a terrible thing, Robin, to be in love with two men at once. When I looked at Barnabas, I saw my future, everything we could have together. But Erasmus was the past, my past. That's a very difficult force to resist. He'd changed, but inside, he was still the boy I knew my whole life. We kissed for the first time under the Wishing Tree. The moon was full and the moths were in flight. We'd spent the afternoon walking around the coast, Barnabas had been struck by his muse and had to work while he could. I don't know why I did it. It just...felt right. But Erasmus was wracked with guilt. The next morning he left in *Bucca's Call* and I didn't see him again for another two years."

"'E made an 'abit of runnin' away from 'is problems," Robin said. "Maybe that's where I get it from."

Morwenna nodded. "By the time he'd come back, Barnabas and I had realised we'd never have children. It was a difficult time for us. He'd wanted to be a father so badly. Erasmus and I, we picked up where we left off. I couldn't control myself. I know it's pathetic; I know it's not right, but I couldn't. Something had changed in him. He wasn't scared anymore. He knew what he wanted."

Morwenna had begun to cry again now. Robin raced to her side. He knelt by her and took her hand in his. Much of this he'd already known from Erasmus's journal, but hearing it from Morwenna's side made it more real for him.

"Finding out we'd never have children of our own, it was so hard to accept, and seeing Erasmus again, it was all too much. He'd take me out around the islands at sunset, in *Bucca's Call*. The sea would blaze in these incredible colours. He showed me the edge of the world. The edge of my world."

Thinking of his father deliberately pursuing a married woman made Robin uncomfortable. It was an act that fell far short of the ideal he'd always held his father to. Whatever his feelings about how he'd been abandoned, Robin had always thought of Erasmus as a fundamentally good and honourable man, but between all of this and finding out he was a pirate, it was a notion that had well and truly been quashed.

"You read 'is journal. You knew 'e were a pirate," Robin said.

"Yes, though he never spoke about it at the time. And before you ask, I didn't know about the Battle in the Bay or the *Caldera*. I didn't know it was really a pirate ship."

"Were you ever going to tell me the truth?" he asked. "You could have at least told me about the piracy."

"How could I? You idolised your father. When he left, I thought you'd never recover. And if you were to lose the picture you'd built of him as well? I couldn't do that to you, not when you were so young."

"I'm a lot older than I used to be," Robin said, forcing a little smile with his pale lips. He could see she was choosing her words carefully, as though she knew that a sharp, ill-chosen word could easily shatter him.

"I feel cheated. I was going to tell you everything. When I was at your bedside in the Moth & Moon, after you collapsed, I planned it all out. I was going to invite you round to my house and tell you what really happened; I was going to give you his journal. But you got to it first. So many times, I'd wanted to confide in you, and just when I'd finally plucked up the courage, the rug was pulled from under me. It was too quick, too brutal, and much too public."

"'Ow did you not realise you were pregnant?" Robin asked. "I mean, I know this isn't exactly my area of expertise, but couldn't you tell?"

Morwenna laughed at this through her tears.

"I don't know what to tell you. It happens sometimes, Robin. It happened to one of my aunties. She got quite a shock one morning in the middle of a sewing circle." They both laughed at this. It felt good; it felt like before.

"I'm going to 'ave to stand up now, because my knee is absolutely killin' me," Robin said as he clambered to his feet. Every joint in his legs popped and cracked as he got up. "I know why you didn't tell Barnabas. I understand what it would 'ave done to 'im. You gave me up for 'im. For the both of you."

It was easy to see why no one had guessed their true relationship. He towered over her, broad-shouldered and formerly blond, with soft, round features. She was short and had been dark in her youth with sharp eyes and nose. Robin took after his father.

"That's...that's not exactly true..." Morwenna began and stopped. "Or maybe it is. I've never thought about it in quite that way before. You said your father ran away from his problems, and that's where you got it from. Well, I do it too, in a way. I waited too long to stop things with Erasmus. I waited too long to tell you the truth. And you do it, too. I see it in you. You wait for things to happen, wait for problems to fix themselves. Wait for other people to make the first move."

She raised her eyebrows at this and he knew what she was getting at. "What are you waiting for, Robin?"

Chapter Twenty-Four

THE VILLAGE WAS a hive of activity. People worked tirelessly to repair the damage caused by the hurricane. Eva and Iris insisted their house staff tend to the needs of their own families and properties before worrying about the relatively minor damage sustained at Wolfe-Chase Lodge.

It was just approaching sunset when they arrived at number 5 Anchor Rise.

"Ladies Wolfe-Chase, thank you so much for comin'," Robin said as he opened his sky-blue front door.

"Thank you for inviting us," Iris said cheerfully. "Was there something in particular you wanted to discuss?"

Eva pulled off her elegant velvet gloves. She was dressed in a deep purple taffeta dress, which swished noisily as she moved. Iris was wearing a more modestly styled floral cotton dress, the same hue as Robin's door.

"There was. Please, come in, come in," he beckoned, leading his guests into his living room.

The fire blazed in the hearth and cast a cosy glow around the room. On her way in, Eva took in the surroundings of Robin's home. Though she lived only a few doors away, she had never been inside before. The house was warm and inviting, and its narrow hallway didn't feel cramped, as she had imagined, but more like a friendly embrace. She looked up to the first floor landing and saw the striking portrait of Captain Erasmus Shipp. She felt his ghost was watching over her, waiting to see what she would do next. Mrs. Whitewater was sitting on an armchair by the fireside in the living room and greeted the women cordially.

"May I offer you both some tea?" Robin asked.

"Actually, Mr. Shipp, if this is about what I suspect it's about, we might be better off with something a bit stronger," Eva said.

"Fair point. I'll get the good stuff," he said as he unlatched his cabinet and removed four small glasses. "And you can call me by my first name, you know. We're not fancy 'ere."

"Sorry, Robin," Eva said, the name still sounding odd on her lips. "Force of habit."

From a decanter, he poured some whiskey and handed one each to his visitors, beckoning them to sit on the settee while he plonked himself on the vacant armchair. "And while we're at it, you can call 'er Morwenner."

Morwenna caught Eva's attention and playfully rolled her eyes as she sipped from her tumbler. "Mrs. Greenaway told me it was you who Sylvia Farriner overheard speaking of Erasmus Shipp's pirate past."

"Ah, yes. I'm sorry about that, I hadn't realised she was listening," Eva said, somewhat taken aback.

"Don't worry. I saw how you stood ready to leap to my aid should things with Sylvia turn physical. I won't soon forget that. Not to mention it's because of you we know of Erasmus' heroism in defending the village. For that, I will always be thankful. We both will. Now, what's this all about, Robin?"

"My father's disappearance," he said.

He told them about Erasmus's journal and the letter it contained.

"Dad wrote about that man you mentioned, Oughterlauney," Robin said. "Said 'e were part of 'is crew for a while. Said 'e were a troublemaker, a violent man. 'e kicked 'im off the boat. In your father's records, did you read anythin' about 'im? About what 'e were up to when the Chase Company ships found 'im? Why do you think my dad would sign onto a vessel under 'im?"

Eva thought about this, trying to divine Erasmus's motivations.

"Well, the thing is, we don't know if he actually signed on to be a crewmember. That's a bit of information that seems to have been repeated so often it's become the truth. Usually, if a ship sinks, my father launches a full investigation, but obviously this was an exception. We have none of the *Caldera*'s records. We don't know what your father was doing on board."

She paused there when she saw the growing disappointment in Robin's face. He'd obviously pinned all of his hopes on her possessing some kernel of information that would clear up this one, final mystery.

"Perhaps Captain Oughterlauney had threatened him?" Iris suggested. "We know your father marooned him and stopped him from attacking the island. Maybe he came back here for revenge. Threatened him. Threatened to hurt you, even. Pirates have all sorts of arcane codes of honour and conduct. Your father might well have surrendered himself to save you. Sacrificed himself."

Robin's brow furrowed as he considered this new possibility. In private, Eva would later swear she could actually hear the cogs turning in his mind.

"Morwenna, did you speak to Captain Shipp that night?" Iris asked.

Morwenna nodded. "He was rattled—preoccupied. I stopped him on the road.It was late and we had to talk quickly. He said he was on his way to speak Barnabas. He could have already been threatened by Captain Oughterlauney by that point, I suppose. He was angry, flustered. Frightened, I think. He rushed off away from me. I called to him, but he wouldn't stop. It was the last time I saw him."

Eva wasn't prone to affectionate displays and was surprised by the urge she felt to hug Morwenna, who looked so very forlorn at that moment. She knew it would be inappropriate, although she suspected it would be secretly welcomed.

"How do we know he went to the *Caldera*?" Eva said, breaking the moment.

"He was seen by the lighthouse keeper at the time," Morwenna said. "He watched him rowing out to the ship. They raised anchor and sailed off as soon as he was on board."

"Dad left a will with 'is journal. 'E must 'ave thought 'e might not be comin' back. Those last few lines 'e wrote, they were different—scratchy. It must have all 'appened so quick, 'e didn't get time to write it down in detail. I think you're right, Iris. Oughterlauney must 'ave threatened 'im. Maybe that's what 'e and Barnabas Whitewater were really arguing over. In 'is letter, Dad said 'e were going "to put an end to this." Maybe 'e meant put an end to the feud between 'im and Oughterlauney? Barnabas probably tried to stop 'im, and that's why they fought?"

Robin looked at Eva with bright, hopeful eyes. She could see how Robin wanted so desperately to find some redeeming quality in his father, some justification for his actions, some noble reason for abandoning him.

"I'm sure that's correct, Mr. Shipp," she said, slipping into formality out of habit and a desperate desire to sound sincere.

"Dad went to the *Caldera* to stop Oughterlauney, but before 'e could, your company's boats found them. If they'd attacked Oughterlauney sooner, if they 'adn't waited...What was it, a matter of a few 'ours? The time it took for Thomas Oughterlauney to come to the island, threaten Dad, and then sail toward Blackrabbit? A few 'ours earlier and Oughterlauney would 'ave been sunk before settin' foot in Blashy Cove. A few 'ours earlier and I'd still 'ave Dad. Just a few 'ours and everythin' would've been different. Everythin' would've been better."

Robin had pitched in wherever he could—helping to fix the schoolhouse, recovering personal items scattered by the winds, and assisting with any other odds and ends that needed doing. He even helped remove the wreckage of boats from the beach. Everyone said they thought he'd avoid seeing the remains of Bucca's Call, but he defiantly cleared up all the parts, ready for disposal. Regardless of how much it pained him, he refused to wait for someone else to do it.

Most of his time had been spent working on the roof of Morwenna's cottage. The basic framework was in place already, and thatching had begun. When it became too dark to work outside, he'd set about fixing the floorboards in his own home, and giving them a new coat of paint. He had also, along with some other men from the village, offered his service to the Trease family to aid in the recovery of their water wheel at the farm. Straddling the stream, it had acted as a filter, catching all of the soil and mud washed down from the hills. It had taken half a day to dig it out, but once it had been moved into the courtyard, the farm's carpenters could begin the job of repairing it.

Robin stood on the first floor landing of his home with his father's journal clasped in his hand. He faced the portrait of Captain Erasmus Shipp, the painting he passed by every day, and saw it through new eyes. At several feet high, it had loomed large in his life, in more ways than one. It used to be a painting of a hero, of an idol—but now it was a painting of a philanderer, and a pirate, and above all, a man. Just a man.

Eva and Iris had stayed only a short while, and Robin had assured them he bore no ill will towards them for the actions of Eva's father.

Morwenna had gone to bed, leaving Robin alone. Brooding wasn't in his nature, but this evening, he found himself unable to do much else. At times like this, his instinct was to cast off in *Bucca's Call* and clear his mind on the open sea. He felt the loss of his silly old boat now more than ever, and far more than he felt able to let on, for how could he voice that particular sentiment now, with everything else going on? It was foolish of him to even be thinking of it. Feeling frustrated, he stuffed the journal into his overcoat, grabbed a lantern, and stormed out of his tall, thin house.

It was late, but there was a murmur of activity coming from the Moth & Moon. Robin walked right past it and made straight for the pier. Stomping along the whole length of it, he sat at the farthest end, dangling his legs over the edge like he used to do when he was a boy. He set the lantern down next to him, and it wasn't long before it attracted a couple of tiny brown moths who flittered around it, trying in vain to break through the brass-and-glass enclosure to the dancing flame within. After the hurricane, the water level had retreated to its usual height, and in the inky blackness of night, the waves were discernible only where they were touched by the moonlight—a scattered reflection, endlessly shifting. A delicate, pale arm stretching out to the horizon.

He reached into his pocket and withdrew the journal. Undoing the leather strap, he flicked through it with his stubby, square fingers, opened it to a random page and began reading. Here, by the gentle lapping sea, his father's voice came ringing across the years, clear as a bell.

"It's been a hard few years. There has been much turmoil and strife. Much suffering and loss, but it will all have been worth it, for it was all for my son."

Robin closed the journal, sat for a while, breathing in the cold, crisp, salty air, and watched the moon sink slowly into the sea.

Chapter Twenty-Five

EDWIN WAS BACK at work in his bakery. While he wished he was getting stuck in with the repair work, the fact remained the people of the village needed food, so people like himself, Mr. Blackwall, Mr. Bounsell, and others were needed back at their businesses. Aside from those that had been levelled, most the buildings on Hill Road and Ridge Street suffered only minor damage. The village's other oysterman, Mr. Hirst, had made a full recovery and already resumed his fishing activities in the cove.

Duncan had been at his toyshop collecting some tools. His shop was undamaged by the hurricane but remained closed while more important matters were dealt with. He'd been working day and night preparing frames, joists, and posts. With all of the trees brought down by the storm, timber was easy to come by. On his way home, he called in to Farriner's Bakery and invited Edwin round to his house that evening. Edwin, somewhat flabbergasted, said he'd be delighted.

When Edwin arrived, it was just getting dark. The sky was still cloudy, and a light rain fell. As he walked up the laneway towards Duncan's little house on the hill, with a wrapped fruitcake in his hand, he spotted a moth fluttering among the hedgerow. With its brilliant blue wings it looked just like the one Robin had told him he'd seen huddling for shelter in the framework of the lighthouse gallery. He'd never seen one like it.

"Thank you for coming," Duncan said as he hung up Edwin's coat.

"I brought you something. Freshly baked this afternoon," Edwin said, handing over the parcel.

Duncan thanked him again and ushered him into the comfortable living room. On a table against the far wall were four model lighthouses in varying stages of completion. Edwin picked up the one on the end, as it was the only one painted—in blue and white stripes—and it looked the sturdiest. Duncan arrived in, carrying a tray loaded with a teapot, butter dish, and two china cups.

"Twist the key on the bottom," he said.

Edwin turned the model over in his hand and gave the little metal key a few turns. Setting the lighthouse back on the table, a simple melody began to play—he recognised it as being the one Robin sometimes hummed. He also saw an occasional little flash of light coming from the top of the model, and he bent down to inspect it.

"It's just a tiny mirror. It glints as it turns and catches the light. Albert Wolfe helped me with the mechanism. Took a few goes to get it right." Duncan smiled.

"I'm sure they'll be very popular," Edwin said.

"I want you to have the first one. By way of an apology."

"That's very kind of you, but really, there's no need."

As he was beckoned to sit on the comfortable armchair by the fireplace, Edwin became aware he was being watched by two bright blue eyes. Bramble the kitten meowed from under Duncan's chair. Edwin called him over, and the little kitten wobbled his way across the carpet to the waiting hands of the baker.

"I believe there is," Duncan said and he sat down. "I was very harsh on you in the lighthouse."

"Oh, no, you weren't..." Edwin began.

Duncan held up his hand. "No, I was, and we both know I was. It wasn't a pleasant time for me, as you can imagine. I did you a great injustice. I thought you were sticking your oar in where it didn't belong, with me and Robin, but you were right to. We needed to talk, and you gave us the push we required. I felt very guilty when I heard what had happened with Robin, rescuing little May Bell. I know now that's why you were so worried about him."

Edwin began to blush a little at this. Duncan's bluntness had disarmed him again. He was used to people skirting around issues, easing into them. Duncan, like Eva, had a way of just ploughing right through them. Edwin wondered if it was a habit he'd picked up when he was living on Blackrabbit Island. He also wondered if perhaps it wasn't a better approach.

"And you know that's not the only reason I was worried," Edwin said.

Duncan smiled at this as he poured two cups of tea and sliced some fruitcake.

"At least we've spoken now. We can move on, as friends. And we have you to thank."

Edwin didn't know what to say. He looked at the carved ornaments on the mantelpiece. He lifted a little bird with a bright spot of red paint on its breast.

"This is the robin you mentioned, from your childhood?" he asked, and Duncan chuckled.

"Yes, that's the one."

Edwin turned it over in his hands, admiring the craftsmanship.

"Have you two talked yet?" Duncan asked.

Edwin coughed slightly, and as he sat back down, he reached over and lifted a cup and saucer.

"Um, no, not yet. We've both been busy, and after the lighthouse, I wondered if maybe you two were..." He was uncertain of how to phrase his thoughts.

"Oh, my, no. No, no, no. You've nothing to worry about there," Duncan said, holding both hands up this time, as if to prove they were clean or just empty. "We've aired our grievances, and we're all the better for it, but that part of our lives is over. Too much water under that particular bridge. He clearly cares a great deal about you."

"Really?" Edwin smiled his biggest, sappiest smile at this.

"You must realise the gamble you're taking with your friendship, though."

"I do. Whatever misgivings I'd had about taking a chance with him were left behind in those caves. On the boat ride back, I had a moment of clarity. I thought sure it was obvious what I was thinking, but Robin was oblivious, as usual! But it just struck me—he's worth the risk."

"He is," Duncan agreed. "But don't tell him I said so or I'll have to thump you."

They laughed then. Was it the first time they'd shared a laugh together, Edwin wondered.

"Look, I know it didn't end well between me and him, but don't let that affect you." Duncan slathered a slice of fruit cake with butter and took a small bite. Edwin fought the urge to tell him his fruit cake was already quite moist enough and didn't require butter.

"I remember once we went out in *Bucca's Call*," Duncan said, wiping a little dab of butter from the corner of his mouth. "Robin had this thing made—it was a few bits of wood, like a little platform that fit snugly over the first two benches of the boat. It was a beautiful summer's evening and we lay on the platform, anchored way out in the bay, watching the clouds. Just me and him. I lay there in his arms, listening to the waves, the birds, the beat of his heart in his chest, and I felt so...at peace. The past, my past, felt like another country. So far away. We watched the sun setting, then the most beautiful starry night. We made wishes on falling stars. He had blankets ready for when it turned cold; he had wine, bread, cheese. It was...perfect, really."

Duncan stopped there, rubbing the back of his own hairy neck with a stubby hand, and let out a little laugh. "I know how it sounds, really, I do," he continued. "But I promise you, I'm not still in love with Robin. I just..."

Edwin held his cup tightly in his hands and felt the intensity of Duncan's gaze. That time, though, it was different. Unlike in the lighthouse, when he was made to feel as if he was intruding on some very private territory, it was more like he being seen—really, truly *seen*—on his own terms. Not as an interloper in Duncan's world, but as a welcomed guest.

"Between you and me, I pine for our relationship in its best days." Duncan said. "I miss *that* Robin. And I miss *that* version of myself. The one finally free of my past."

Bramble had scuttled out from underneath a chair and began trilling and pawing at Duncan's leg. He bent down and scooped up the little kitten, who began to purr instantly. "At least I've got some company round the house now. Even if he never shuts up for five bleddy minutes." He stroked under Bramble's chin.

They talked about how Keeper Hall, recovered from his injuries, had told the village about signalling for help from the lighthouse window for only a few minutes before becoming too disorientated to continue. It was sheer luck that Duncan had seen it.

And they talked about how odd it was that Mr. Reed smiled so much now, when they weren't previously sure it was something he was even capable of doing. They had never before seen his perfect little white teeth, or the way his eyebrows rose in the middle of his forehead and slanted over his slate-coloured eyes.

After a couple of hours swapping stories—more than a few of which concerned Robin—Edwin held his model lighthouse up and waved farewell to Duncan from the laneway. The toymaker stood in the doorway of his little blue house on the hill, framed by the golden warmth of his candlelit hallway and holding in his arms the bright-eyed Bramble. He and Edwin parted if not quite yet as friends, then at least with a better understanding of one another and a solid foundation on which to build.

Chapter Twenty-Six

ROBIN WAS WORKING on the roof of Morwenna's cottage and the repairs were nearing completion. It was a clean and crisp morning, and the smell of brine filled the air. The bright sunshine—a welcome relief after the gloom of the previous few days—was turning his broad, bare back slightly pink in tone, and his massive, brawny shoulders were beginning to sting a little. Beads of sweat gathered on his brow and he wiped them away with his meaty forearm as he carefully sat back against the chimneystack. Pulling his cap down farther over his eyes to shield them from the sun, he heard a familiar voice call up to him.

"Mr. Shipp! Can you come down for a minute?"

He looked down to see little May Bell excitedly jumping around.

"Right now? I'm almost done 'ere. Can it wait a while?" he said.

"No, it's got to be right now!" May replied, barely able to contain herself.

Robin laughed as he clambered down to the garden, wiping his hands on his breeches.

"Now, what's so urgent?" he asked as lifted his shirt from the fence.

He pulled it on and began to button it closed. His thick fingers made this task a bit fiddly, and he was taking entirely too long for the child's liking. Before he had the third button fastened over his hefty belly, May had grabbed Robin by one burly forearm and began to drag him away.

"Come along!" she called. "Hurry!"

She dragged Robin the whole way to the harbour where seemingly the entire village had gathered. Edwin was there and was deep in conversation with Morwenna. Dr. Greenaway and his wife, Mr. Bounsell, Mr. Reed, and Mr. Blackwall were all there, as were the Ladies Wolfe-Chase, with the blacksmith and his sons. Jim, Arabella, and Allister Stillpond were present, and May's parents too. Her father, Henry, was propped up on a couple of wooden crutches, his ankle still in bandages. Even Mrs. Kind and the tweed knights could be seen mingling among the crowd. They were all talking excitedly and they cheered and laughed when they beheld the sight of the little girl trailing the huge fisherman by the arm. Robin was stumbling to keep up.

"What's all this, now?" He laughed when he reached the crowd and was finally freed from the youngster's grasp. He absent-mindedly closed the rest of the buttons on his shirt, but used too much force on the last one, causing it to pop off and bounce away across the cobblestones towards the beach. Edwin caught it underfoot and picked it up. He stepped forward and tucked the button into the pocket of Robin's shirt.

"Well, Mr. Shipp," he said to the crowd as much as to Robin. "You've been working nonstop to help everyone fix their homes and businesses and get back on their feet, and, well, we all thought you deserved something in return."

He placed his hand on Robin's sunburned shoulder, causing him to wince ever so slightly, and turned him around to face one of the big sheds by the shore. Sitting on the roof were the Admiral and Captain Tom, still squawking and bickering. They had survived the hurricane seemingly unscathed.

The doors of the big red shed slowly opened and so did Robin's eyes. He raced over and touched the prow, to make sure it was real. He traced his hand along the hull, across the beautifully vivid scarlet paint, and over the nameplate, with every letter lovingly painted on. He could hardly believe it. There, standing on blocks of wood, paintwork gleaming in the sun stood the fully restored *Bucca's Call*. He turned to face the crowd with tears in his eyes.

"But 'ow..." he began.

He couldn't begin to express what he was feeling. This boat wasn't just a gift from his father, wasn't just a link to his past, it was also—he had recently discovered—his birthplace.

Edwin held his hands up. "Everyone wanted to help. But it wasn't just us, this was Duncan's idea. He did most of the work."

He pointed to the toymaker, who appeared sheepishly from the other side of the vessel.

"I couldn't have done it without help," Duncan said.

Morwenna chirped up. "He spent every spare moment repairing her."

"'Ow did you do this without me noticin'?" Robin exclaimed.

"It wasn't easy," Duncan said. "We thought for sure you'd want to stay away from the dock for a while, but you were here, helping clear away the wrecks. We sneaked down here one night and moved the remnants of *Bucca* into the shed."

"I had to dig in the wet sand by candlelight. It was awful," said Ben Blackwall, "but worth it." He corrected himself when he realised how it sounded.

"But she were in pieces..." Robin said.

"Yes, well, like I said, everyone pitched in," said Duncan, gesturing to the assembled crowd.

Robin had quite lost the run of himself and was dabbing his eyes and nose with a big linen handkerchief he had pulled from his back pocket. He tucked it away again and, still sniffling and smiling, he loomed over Duncan and hugged the toymaker off his feet.

"I can never repay you for this kindness, Duncan. Thank you," Robin said as he set him back down again.

Bramble walked along the edge of the boat and meowed loudly, pawing at Robin's arm when he saw Duncan being hoisted. Robin laughed and held out a chunky finger to the kitten, who cautiously licked it before rubbing his face against it.

"Don't worry, little 'un, I won't 'urt 'im," he said.

The force of Robin's hug had dislodged Duncan's many-lensed glasses from his nose, and he smiled as he fixed them back into place.

"You should thank Edwin," he said. "He's the one who rallied the village."

"Oh, I'll thank 'im properly; don't you worry!" Robin replied with a cheeky wink.

And deep inside, down in the pit of his stomach, down in the vault of his soul, Robin felt the knot begin to unravel.

Chapter Twenty-Seven

EDWIN WAS IN the backyard of his bakery. He'd wheeled a large cart down the laneway by the side of the building and was busy loading it up with rubbish leftover from the storm. There were still plenty of scraps from trees lying around, as well as bits of straw, glass, and wood left over from the repairs. Parts of the destroyed buildings a couple of doors up had found their way into his yard, too. Bricks and chunks of plaster littered the ground. Edwin, knowing this would be a messy job, had dressed in his oldest clothes. A faded, moth-eaten cotton shirt and chestnut-coloured corduroy fall-front breeches. He was struggling to chop up a particularly uncooperative piece of broken joist when he heard a friendly greeting from the laneway.

"Evenin', Edwin," called Robin.

He stopped in midswing and turned to greet his friend. "My, my! What's all this about, then?"

Robin was smiling that big dopey smile of his. The one that made his cheeks puff out and his sky-blue eyes twinkle. He was standing with one arm behind his back, wearing a fawn-toned linen suit—which was thoroughly wrinkled and probably had been even before he'd put it on— with a striped cotton shirt and a small muslin cravat, tied in a bow. This all clashed terribly with his trusty navy-coloured cap, which rested—as it always did—on his bulging ears. Edwin didn't think he'd ever seen Robin in anything other than a knitted woollen jumper and overcoat.

"Well," Robin said, "I thought it might be nice to make an effort."

Edwin rubbed his hands clean on his breeches. "You look very dashing I feel thoroughly underdressed."

"Speaking of which, I got you this…" Robin produced from behind his back a package wrapped in paper and tied with twine, which immediately slipped from his grasp and landed in a pile of sawdust on the ground.

"Ah, bleddy useless fingers. Sorry..." He started to bend down to retrieve it, but Edwin beat him to it, and he lifted the parcel. While a great deal of time had been spent preparing this, it was clear Robin had wrapped it himself. The paper was rumpled and torn where it had been wrapped and rewrapped, and the string frayed where it had been snapped by hand instead of cut. Edwin opened it and found inside a new cream-coloured linen shirt. Identical to the one that had been torn in the caves.

"Oh, Robin, you didn't have to do this. It's much too expensive," he said, hugging the fisherman. He didn't have the heart to tell him he'd already repaired the other shirt and didn't need another one.

Robin laughed and bent down to pick up the axe. With one easy swing of his arm, he cleaved the stubborn block of wood in two, squinting to avoid the splinters flying in every direction, and tossed the logs into the cart.

"Least I could do since I ruined the other one. The market traders have started comin' back to the village. I 'ope it'll fit you," he said, looking around. "I didn't realise there 'ad been so much damage round 'ere."

"There wasn't, really. Most of this was just blown in from elsewhere. Do you want to come up for a drink? I'm just finishing up now, anyway. It's getting dark."

In Edwin's lodgings above the bakery, they sat facing one another on a long, worn settee, leaning against the scrolled arms and resting their elbows on the low serpentine back. Robin had removed the jacket to his suit and already loosened the cravat, which now hung open around his neck. He popped open the first few buttons of his shirt, as it was tight around his staunch neck. "Now I remember why I never wear things like this," he said.

Edwin's living room was painted turquoise and had two windows made up of small, lead-lined panes facing onto Hill Road. Between these sat a shallow bay window, similarly paned. On the windowsills sat two copper candelabra, ornately sculpted to look like leaves that had been twisted and pulled into a standing position. It was dusk now, and the candlelight turned the windows into faint mirrors.

The settee sat against a wall, facing these dim reflectors. On another wall was a pot-bellied stove, which currently held a blazing fire and gently warmed the whole quarters. There was almost no art to be found, save for a small, simple charcoal drawing of his late brother, which hung on the wall in a plain frame between his bedroom and bathroom. Ambrose had looked very similar to his younger brother, except he managed to have a full head of hair. A model of the Merryapple lighthouse—Duncan's gift—sat on a table by the windows.

His lodgings were clean and homely, but slightly ramshackle. Everything was just a little bit frayed around the edges and off-kilter. He worked long hours and found it hard to find time for the upkeep of his home. More than once, he'd arrived back, kicked the boots off his tired feet, and fallen asleep on this faded olive sofa. Being positioned above the bakery, his home had a permanent aroma of freshly baked bread. Robin often remarked that each time he visited he thought it smelled like home.

In the flickering candlelight, they were keenly aware this was the first time they'd been alone together since the lighthouse.

"How are things between you and Morwenna?" Edwin asked as he handed a small glass of whiskey to Robin.

Robin took a deep breath. "I don't know; it's so...complicated. When I were a lad, I used to dream about Dad coming back with Rose. That 'e'd left to find 'er and bring 'er back to Blashy Cove, so we could be a family. Now I find out there is no Rose—there never was. That maybe Morwenner and Dad could 'ave... I don't know. I wish I could talk to 'im."

Robin spoke of the Wolfe-Chase's visit and the conclusions they had all reached. Edwin's heart went out to him. He'd gone through so much in the past few days—he'd found his mother and lost his father. Again. Lost the version he'd built up in his mind, at least. He wished he could do something to help, but he knew all he could offer was a sympathetic ear and a shoulder to cry on. Robin sat back in his seat and took a sip of whiskey.

"I think I'm grievin' for Rose. Isn't that silly? With everythin' else goin' on, I'm grievin' for a woman who never existed. But I thought she did, you see. I felt like she did. I imagined 'er leavin' me in *Bucca's Call*. I imagined 'er sailin' back to Blackrabbit under the cover of darkness. I wondered what 'er life there was like. If she 'ad an 'usband. Other children. I built a whole life for 'er in my mind. In my 'eart," he said, tapping his chest with a bulky, clenched fist.

"I wondered if she thought about me at all. And then, all of a sudden, she were gone. Now, don't get me wrong, I'd rather 'ave a real mother than an imaginary one, but inside, you see, inside it felt like I'd lost someone real."

Edwin nodded. He understood. He could see the heartache written on Robin's face, living in his eyes. Duncan was right—Robin was an open book. They sat in silence for a while, absorbing what he'd said. Letting it all sink in.

"How is she coping?" Edwin said at last.

"She's been very quiet. It's all been too much for 'er. She said she 'ad made up 'er mind to tell me, but I got there first. Blindsided 'er. It's funny; I were blindsided myself, in the light'ouse."

Edwin furrowed his brow and thought back.

"I didn't mean to..." he started, but Robin cut him off.

"You couldn't 'ave known, but when I was lyin' in bed in the Moth & Moon, I 'ad made up my mind to talk to Duncan, to try to clear the air between us. At long last."

"But I forced you to do it before you were ready." Edwin realised.

Robin rubbed his earlobe and sat back in his seat. "You did. And to be 'onest, for a minute there—just a minute, mind—I were mad at you for doin' it. It were all for the best, in the end, but I do wish I'd 'ad more time to prepare."

"Robin, I'm sorry, I never meant to... You know that I would never..."

Robin smiled at him. "I know; don't worry. What about you? What 'appened with your mum?" Robin swigged from the glass.

"We got a letter from her yesterday. Well, I did, anyway. She's gone back to Blackrabbit Island to live with her sister. It seems they were hit worse by the hurricane than we were. Many of the buildings in her sister's town were damaged or outright destroyed. It will be a long time before they recover. I don't think she'll ever come back here, though."

"I bet your dad's glad to 'ear that."

"He's coping surprisingly well. I swear he's healthier and more alert than he's been in years. Freed from under her thumb, he's even walking a little straighter. I feel so sorry for her, though. I know what she did was wrong, but, well, she's my mum.

"I still can't believe she knew this whole time. She knew Barnabas Whitewater fell. Morwenner told me somethin' else, mind," Robin said, tugging his ear again. "That night, she'd told Dad they couldn't see each other anymore. And it made 'im angry."

"It still doesn't mean he pushed Mr. Whitewater. Maybe he was angry, and maybe he did tell Barnabas the truth—there probably was a scuffle of some kind—but Barnabas still fell. It was still an accident. You spent your whole life thinking your dad was a certain way. It'll take some time to adjust to thinking of him as he really was."

Robin took another drink. "I suppose you're right."

"Oh, there's something else," Edwin said.

Robin visibly braced himself. "I've come to strongly dislike those words."

"I've taken May Bell on as my apprentice. I spoke to her mother a couple of days ago. She'd wanted more responsibility than just running bread all over the village. She was always trying to help, trying to do more for me. She's got a lot to learn, but she's smart and determined. I think she'll do well. You and Eva were right."

"Always listen to your elders." Robin laughed.

"Don't let Eva hear you call her that," Edwin warned. "I think it'll make a difference, having some help around the bakery. I'm sure you've noticed, but I haven't been happy recently. To tell the truth, I was beginning to feel like I was haunting my own life. Just a pale shadow, going through the motions. Duncan invited me round to his home last night, and he helped me put things in perspective."

"Really? That's a surprise. I didn't think you two were that close," Robin replied.

"We're not, well, not really. At least, we never were before."

"What did you talk about?" Robin asked, taking another sip from his glass.

"You, mostly." Edwin smiled.

"Oh dear, I dread to think what 'e said about me," Robin said, pulling an exaggerated face.

"You do him a disservice. He still cares for you, in his own way."

"I still care for 'im as well. If I didn't, I wouldn't 'ave found it so 'ard to talk to 'im in the light'ouse."

"I must admit, I always thought he was a bit...cold. But I've gotten to know him better. He's just...guarded, I suppose is the word. I've seen his softer side now, though. He's sentimental, I think. More sentimental than he'd have you believe," Edwin said, eyeing the toy lighthouse. "He kept the wooden robin from his childhood. He kept the coat you bought him."

He thought about mentioning the note he'd seen fall from Duncan's pocket in the lantern room, but decided it wasn't his place to do so.

"I think he's afraid of losing everything again, so he holds on to the good things. Even if they're tainted, tinged with sadness, they're still worth holding on to for the good things they represent. The better times. He's lost so much in the past—his childhood home, his family, the life he built for himself on Blackrabbit Island. I think he sees the value in the little things."

As he spoke, he could see Robin mulling his words over in his mind. The big man's kindly, sky-blue eyes moved slowly from side to side. They were a little brighter now, a little less sad, he thought. His gaze flickered across Robin's form. How different he looked in those clothes, how dapper. The expensive linen of his suit, far finer than the workaday cloth he would usually wear, draped his titanic form in subtly seductive ways that Robin was, naturally, completely oblivious to, but which Edwin couldn't help but admire. The gathers and folds of it, the peaks and troughs.

"Duncan gave me one bit of advice," Edwin continued. "He told me to hold your hand as often as I can because the day will come when I won't be able to, and there'll be nothing in this world I'll want more."

"And is it what you want to do?" Robin asked cautiously.

Edwin tilted his head back, recalling the events of the past few days.

"When I was at your bedside after you collapsed, it brought a lot of things back to me. It reminded me of seeing Ambrose on his deathbed, but it also...it made me think about what would happen if you died. What I would have missed out on. I thought I was falling for you a long time ago, and I was going to tell you, but then you met Duncan. I put those feelings aside, chalked them up to nothing more than a passing infatuation. And it was fine. Really, it was. We were friends, close friends, and it was enough. But then you were lying there, and I thought you might...well, like I said, it brought a lot of things back."

Edwin's hand rested on the back of his settee, and Robin reached out, laid his weighty, rugged hand on top of it, and gently squeezed. How warm it felt.

They decided some fresh air would be a good idea. Edwin retired to his bathroom, where he splashed some water on his face and under his arms, then returned to the living room where he pulled Robin's gift on over his head. While Robin sat and watched, Edwin let the garment drape over his solid chest and soft belly. It was a perfect fit. He lit a candle inside a lantern, and the two men walked downstairs and out onto Hill Road. It was a beautiful clear night, the stars felt closer than ever, and the moon was almost full. They waved to the people they passed by, and soon they were standing on the cobbled road leading to the Moth & Moon. The great tavern loomed ahead of them—lit by a thousand candles, or so it seemed—with its apex like a mountain summit. The sign had been returned to its rightful place above the door, and the softly-ticking wooden moth had resumed its endless journey. They gazed over to the pier, where *Bucca's Call* swayed happily on the tide. The sea gently crashed against the shore in a hypnotic rush and ebb.

"That sound usually calms my heart," Robin said. "But tonight, it's beating faster than ever."

"Before we go in, Robin," Edwin said nervously, "I wanted to say...this might sound silly, but I hope...I hope what my mother said, what she did, I hope it doesn't affect how you think of me. I hope you know what you mean to me."

Robin tipped his cap back, put one hand on Edwin's waist and the other just under his ear. He carefully pulled him in close, looked into his sea-green eyes, and kissed him. Still holding the little lantern, Edwin put one hand on the side of Robin's big, round face, feeling the softness of his cheek, the strength in his neck.

"That was worth the wait," Edwin whispered.

He lifted one end of Robin's untied cravat, twirling it playfully around the end of his finger.

"Edwin, I've spent a lifetime experiencin' what 'appens when people 'old you to account for someone else's actions. You proved to the whole village that my father didn't kill Barnabas Whitewater. You showed them what really 'appened that night on the 'eadland. You even got me and Duncan talkin', after years of 'eartache. I never thought I'd know this kind of peace."

Framed by the tavern and bathed in moonlight, Robin held Edwin close and kissed him again.

"You saved me." Robin smiled.

The sky blazed red and pink as Robin Shipp and Edwin Farriner lay aboard *Bucca's Call* with nary a stitch between them save for the old, navy-coloured, flat-topped cap, which had decamped from its historic home and claimed temporary sanctuary on Edwin's shaven head. They lay there, using pillows formed from their garments, comfortably sprawled with hands entwined on the platform that nestled across the little boat's benches, watching the sun climb higher and higher.

Robin turned to look at the island. From there, he could see the whole village. Roofs were fixed, windows were replaced, and apart from the missing buildings on the corner of Hill Road, where work on a new museum had already begun, all signs there had ever been a hurricane were gone. But while life was getting back to normal for everyone else, he knew his had changed forever. Sunlight glinted off the brightly painted houses and dazzled on the water as *Bucca's Call*, with her gleaming new hull and pristine sails, gently bobbed on the waves. Before long, Robin's stomach began to rumble.

"Time for food?" Edwin asked, resting his hand on Robin's big, round belly.

"Oh yes," replied Robin, "an' I know just the place to get some!"

About the Author

Glenn Quigley is a graphic designer originally from Dublin and now living in Lisburn, Northern Ireland. He creates bear designs for www.themoodybear.com. He has been interested in writing since he was a child, as essay writing was the one and only thing he was ever any good at in school. When not writing or designing, he enjoys photography and has recently taken up watercolour painting.

Website: www.glennquigley.com

Twitter: @Glennquigley

Also Available from NineStar Press

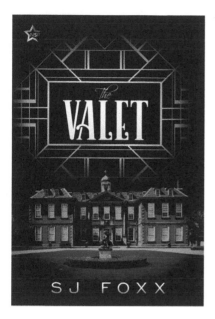

Connect with NineStar Press

www.ninestarpress.com

www.facebook.com/ninestarpress

www.facebook.com/groups/NineStarNiche

www.twitter.com/ninestarpress

www.tumblr.com/blog/ninestarpress